Sisterhood

of

Sleuths

Certainly Nancy Drew never missed an opportunity for a thrilling adventure.

—CAROLYN KEENE,
THE BUNGALOW MYSTERY

Sisterhood
of
Sleuths

Jennifer Chambliss Bertman

WITH ILLUSTRATIONS BY VESPER STAMPER

Christy Ottaviano Books
LITTLE, BROWN AND COMPANY
New York Boston

Text copyright © 2022 by Jennifer Chambliss Bertman
Illustrations copyright © 2022 by Vesper Stamper

Cover art copyright © 2022 by Sarah Watts
Cover design by Sasha Illingworth and Patrick Hulse
Cover copyright © 2022 by Hachette Book Group, Inc.

Christy Ottaviano Books
Hachette Book Group
1290 Avenue of the Americas, New York, NY 10104
Visit us at LBYR.com

First Edition: October 2022

Christy Ottaviano Books is an imprint of
Little, Brown and Company. The Christy Ottaviano Books name
and logo are trademarks of Hachette Book Group, Inc.

The publisher is not responsible for websites (or their content)
that are not owned by the publisher.

Library of Congress Cataloging-in-Publication Data
Names: Bertman, Jennifer Chambliss, author. |
Stamper, Vesper, illustrator.
Title: Sisterhood of sleuths / Jennifer Chambliss Bertman ;
with illustrations by Vesper Stamper.
Description: First edition. | New York ; Boston :
Little, Brown and Company, 2022. | Includes author's note and
bibliographical references. | Audience: Ages 9–14. |
Summary: "When eleven-year-old Maizy finds a box of vintage
Nancy Drew books, her mysterious discovery uncovers a truth
from the past that will lead to self-discovery in the present,
connecting three generations of women." —Provided by publisher.
Identifiers: LCCN 2021056400 | ISBN 9780316331074 (hardcover) |
ISBN 9780316331340 (ebook)
Subjects: CYAC: Books and reading—Fiction. | Friendship—Fiction. |
Drew, Nancy (Fictitious character)—Fiction. | LCGFT: Novels.
Classification: LCC PZ7.1.B46485 Si 2022 | DDC [Fic]—dc23
LC record available at https://lccn.loc.gov/2021056400

ISBNs: 978-0-316-33107-4 (hardcover),
978-0-316-33134-0 (ebook)

Printed in the United States of America

LSC-C

Printing 1, 2022

FOR MY MOM,
WHO SPARKED MY LOVE OF READING,

FOR MOOSIE, WHO GIFTED ME A
CARDBOARD BOX FULL OF NANCY DREWS,

AND FOR CHRISTY OTTAVIANO,
A NANCY DREW KINDRED SPIRIT

❧ CONTENTS ❧

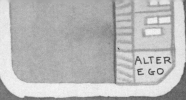

ALTER EGO

MAIZY

NELL

SHOPS

LIBRARY

TURN THE PAGE

JACUZZI

MAIN STREET

LARKSVILLE MIDDLE SCHOOL

AUDREY

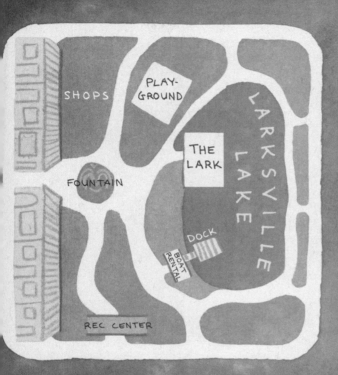

SCOOPS

THE CURIO

LARKSVILLE COLLEGE

CAFÉ

SHOPS

PLAY-GROUND

THE LARK

LARKSVILLE LAKE

FOUNTAIN

DOCK

BOAT RENTAL

ANNETTE

REC CENTER

LARKSVILLE

1

An Unexpected Delivery

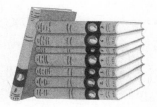

HANGING OUT WITH IZZY LATELY HAS BEEN LIKE PUTTING ON A FAVORITE sweatshirt that doesn't feel quite right. Like maybe it shrank in the dryer, or a seam has begun to unravel. So when Izzy calls to see if Mom and I need extra help at the shop this morning, I'm too surprised to wonder why.

"You want to help?" I repeat.

Izzy hates spending time at Alter Ego. It's a vintage store, and she's convinced some things are haunted just because they came from deceased owners. Like the floral-painted handheld mirror that's been in the shop for over a year. She refuses to go near it because she says our spirits will get trapped inside if we look at our reflection.

Izzy is dramatic that way. It's one of the things I love about her, and one of the things that kind of bugs me too.

"I know it's the busy season," Izzy says.

Which is true. In addition to vintage odds and ends, Alter Ego rents costumes. But not the cheap kind you can buy in a bag from a party store. These are true period pieces, castoffs from old stage productions, and really nice homemade outfits. September and October are always busy months for Mom, with people renting costumes for Halloween and homecoming events.

"We can go to Scoops when we're done," Izzy suggests.

This makes me pause. Ice cream on a Saturday morning in the middle of September isn't the sort of thing she would normally want to do. But Scoops is where my brother works—at least for a few more days, until he goes to college—and Izzy and I did go there sometimes over the summer. If there wasn't anyone else in the shop, Max gave us free ice cream and we had the arcade games in the back all to ourselves. I really want to believe this is Izzy, the old Izzy, eager to hang out and be our normal selves together.

"Sure," I say. "And we can make plans for *Shellfish Holmes*. We need to figure out the rest of the plot."

"What's to figure out?" Before I can answer, Izzy reverses course, her voice turning a corner from annoyed to fake calm. "Sure, Maizy. We can talk about your movie."

"*Our* movie," I say, in case part of the awkwardness between us is that she doesn't feel like I include her enough.

Izzy and I make plans to meet at Alter Ego in an hour. I whistle while I lace my shoes, trying not to think about how she snubbed me at school yesterday. Izzy said she didn't. Maybe she didn't. She probably didn't.

I keep whistling.

"You're in a good mood," Dad says as he helps load stuff into the back of Mom's car.

"It's going to be a great day," I say.

And I almost believe it.

⌒⌒⌒

The parking lot behind Alter Ego is mostly empty this early on a Saturday. It's just me, Mom, and the cars of people in the yoga studio that's on the third floor of the old building that houses her shop. Alter Ego is on the ground level, and the second floor has private offices for people who usually aren't here on the weekend.

"Can you carry that?" Mom raises an elbow to point at a shopping bag in the wayback of our SUV. Her hands are full with a large shadow-box-like frame my dad built to display marbles in the store window. I grab the bag—it's filled with quilts Mom must be adding to the store's collection, and on top of those rests a plastic tub of the marbles that will fill the frame.

As we cross the parking lot, I'm mulling over the problem with my movie plot.

"Do you think it matters *how* somebody dies? Or just that they died?" I ask Mom.

She pauses mid-step to boost the frame up with her knee. "Of course it matters. It matters to the people who love the person."

"But would it matter to you in a story? Or a movie? Do you need to know how the character died, or just that they're dead?"

Mom considers this as she rests the frame against the building and unlocks the back door. "I guess it depends on the story. If it's about their death, then yes. It would matter a lot."

"That's what I think!"

Mom holds the door open for me as I continue.

"Izzy says it doesn't matter if—"

I step forward like I've done a million times before entering the storeroom at the back of the shop, but this time the lip of wood grabs the toe of my sneaker. I stumble inside, surprised, and launch the bag into the air. It lands with a *plomp*, and the tub falls out. Marbles spill everywhere.

"Maizy, what in the world?" Mom flips on the light switch and looks around as if there's a tripping culprit lurking. Other than the marbles rolling around, the space is tidy as usual. The walls are lined with shelves that hold inventory and supplies organized in orderly bins and baskets, and an empty worktable sits in the middle of the room. Marvin the store cat patters in to investigate.

"Are you okay? What happened?" Mom asks.

"Wood sprites," I reply, scooping up a few of the marbles that Marvin is now batting in every direction. "Pretty sure that was wood sprites."

"Wood sprites?" She shakes her head and laughs. "Too bad those years of ballet lessons didn't help with your clumsiness." She winks and picks up the fallen bag, leaving the marble tub on the floor for me to refill. "I'm going to set up the rest of this stuff."

I call after her as she walks away. "For the record, it was only *months* of ballet! In first grade. And the lessons did help—I trip with style!"

I hear Mom laugh again from the next room as I crawl around, corralling marbles—except for the rainbow-swirl one Marvin is galloping after—and get back to thinking about death. Specifically, the one that happens in *Shellfish Holmes*.

Shellfish Holmes is our latest screenplay—my screenplay, really. I wrote it. But Izzy acted out the dialogue very dramatically, which was helpful too. It's going to star Lois, the stuffed lobster I got as a souvenir when Izzy and I went to the aquarium a couple of summers ago. We always use stuffed animals and toys to cast our movies.

We've been making movies together since third grade. But *Shellfish Holmes* needs to be our best one yet. It's for a group project in language arts. We're supposed to pick a genre—like comedy, mystery, science fiction—and a storytelling method to create an original work. Everybody in class will vote for their favorite (not their own, of course), and the winning project will be shown as part of a school fundraiser at the Curio.

The Curio is an old movie house that was going to be torn down until a bunch of Larksville residents banded together to save it. Now it's been renovated, and the lobby doubles as an art gallery, and the theater has both live concerts and plays and also retro movie nights. Once a month, the feature is a movie made by local teenagers. It's a big deal to have your movie selected, and as soon as I'm old enough, I'm entering my films.

But if *Shellfish Holmes* gets the class vote, then I won't have to wait. I might be the youngest director to have a movie shown at the Curio.

Our script has everything a good mystery needs: *Detective?* Shellfish Holmes. *Mystery setup?* The leading lady of a play mysteriously dies. *Suspects?* The director, a castmate, and a boyfriend (because Izzy says there has to be a boyfriend).

We even know *who did it and why*: It was the castmate, who wanted the lead role for herself. She tries to frame the director for the murder, because he didn't cast her, and she's hoping her boyfriend will become the new director. To help herself look innocent, she's the one to hire Shellfish Holmes in the first place.

It's brilliant! It has everything! Everything except *how* the starlet dies.

Izzy says that doesn't matter; most people won't notice. She says we need to move on from the script and start filming, because we only have two weeks left to work on it. But I say every detail counts. Even if our audience doesn't care, *I* want to know.

I reach for the last marble, but Marvin zooms over, his fluffy butt skidding past me as he paws the marble into the next room.

"Marvin, you're not helping." I crawl into the costume room, but Marvin gets to the marble first. He scampers after it into yet another room, so I stand up, and I'm about to head back to get the marble tub when a loud thud comes from the front of the shop.

"Mom?" I call, at the same time she yells from the quilt room, "Maizy, what happened now?"

"That wasn't me! It's probably Marvin."

It actually sounded more like someone trying to shove open the locked front door. Maybe it's Izzy, even though she knows to come in through the back when the store is closed.

Marvin's at the front, tail swishing, so I expect to see a face in the window, but nobody's there.

Before I do anything else, I scan Main Street. I don't know why, exactly. Maybe with my murder mystery on the brain, I'm on extra-high alert for suspicious things. But it's just the same old shop-lined street, beginning to wake up. Mr. Lim sweeps the sidewalk in front of Scoops, someone from Abuelita's Tacos sets out a fresh bowl of water for dogs, and a couple exits the coffee shop, to-go cups in hand.

Marvin paws at the door and meows. There's a large package of some sort out there. That must have been the thud. I unlock the door and open it, shoving the package far enough away that I can step out. It's a heavy box, and I have to lean into the door to move it.

Marvin brushes past my leg, going outside to rub against a corner of the cardboard.

"Who left this?" I ask him.

Mrow? he replies.

I try to pick up the box, but it's too heavy. I scoot it with the side of my foot, alternating legs as I move it inch by inch until it's just inside and I can close the door. Marvin jumps on top, but the flaps sink and he springs right out. The box wasn't sealed or even addressed.

"Someone left a box of stuff at the front door," I call to Mom. Sometimes people bring in random things to see if Mom wants to buy them.

"Hello?" Izzy's voice wafts from the back room, hesitant and unsure. "Mrs. Turner? Maizy?"

"Izzy-bell!" I leave the box and run to the back. She's still holding the door open, eyeing the shelves around her warily.

"Come on in, the ghosts won't bite," I say.

"Hilarious," Izzy mutters with a roll of her eyes, like that was definitely *not* what she was worried about, but she only takes a baby step inside.

I throw my arms around her and squeeze. "You know I'm teasing, Izzy."

She relaxes, gently removing herself from the hug. "I know. And *you* know I go by Isabelle now."

"Right, right. It's just hard to think of you any other way—you've always been Izzy to me. Isabelle feels like a completely different person, you know?"

She shrugs and says, "Well, around other people, at least, try to remember."

Mom sets us up with freshly laundered costumes that need to be put on hangers and an assortment of collectible tins that need to be stickered. She also wheels the box back on a dolly, dropping it next to my feet with a thud.

"It looks like mostly books in there, but maybe sort through to make sure," she says.

Mom doesn't normally sell books, so whoever left the box either didn't know or didn't care.

"Maybe someone meant to leave this at Turn the Page," she adds. "We'll check with Maureen after you go through the box."

Turn the Page is the bookstore two blocks down. It's a narrow, one-story orange building with a front patio filled with green furniture for story times, squeezed between a ramen place and a bank—very different from Alter Ego, in our tall corner building with white-paned windows and blue-and-white striped awnings. So I doubt it was a mix-up. But I shrug and say, "Sure, I'll look through it."

Izzy opts for the costumes—they probably strike her as less likely to be possessed.

"Let's talk *Shellfish Holmes*," I launch in. As I talk, I lift a flap of the box and remove one old book after another, setting them on the table. "Lois will obviously be the detective, but what should we use for the other characters? Should we stick with a sea-animal theme, or is it funnier if we mix it up?"

Izzy sighs and clips a poodle skirt onto a hanger. "Maizy, this is a school project, and we're sixth graders now. We can't use stuffed animals and dolls. This isn't a silly game."

A silly game? I thunk a book down a little too hard.

When Steven Spielberg made his first feature-length sci-fi movie, *Firelight*, as a teenager, was that a silly game? When Tim Burton filmed his first animated short at thirteen, was that a *silly game*?!

Izzy removes a velvet coat from the dry-cleaning bag and holds it up to the window that faces the parking lot.

"We have to use Lois," I insist. "I wrote the script for her."

Izzy slides her arm into one sleeve. "You can rewrite it."

Rewrite it? *Rewrite it?!*

Like all the work I'd already put into writing the script didn't matter? Like it had been no big deal and I'd just whip up another one with a human detective?

I keep piling book after book onto the table, not even looking at them. Just *thunk, thunk, THUNK.*

WESTERN
SHIRTS

1950'S
DRESSES

"The other day, you said we were taking too long with the story. That we should move on to filming. And besides, the detective *has* to be a lobster. It's *Shellfish* Holmes, remember? That's the whole joke."

I half expect Izzy to point out that clams and crayfish and shrimp are shellfish too, so the detective doesn't *have* to be a lobster. But Izzy doesn't say any of that. Instead, she walks to the costume room to get a view of herself in the full-length mirror. "What if we paired up with Link and Ben?"

"Link?" That's the only word that pops out of my mouth, but my head is full of them. Questions like: *How did we go from arguing about Shellfish Holmes to talking about Link and Ben, and why in the world would we partner with them, anyway, and—*

"Lincoln Diaz. Everybody calls him Link."

"I know who Link is. And Ben too. We're all in the same class. We don't need to partner with them or anyone else. Mr. Orson said just the two of us is fine."

"Maybe it would be more fun. Think about it. We could go see if they're playing arcade games at Scoops later and ask them."

Scoops. *That's* why she wanted to get ice cream. That's why she offered to help this morning. I'm too mad to talk about this anymore. I plunge both hands into the box of books and lift an armload, letting them topple onto the others I've already removed. These books are nearly identical: faded denim-blue covers with dark blue letters and the silhouette of a lady peering through a magnifying glass.

Izzy gasps, and despite myself, I look over. The velvet coat has been hung up, and the next costume she's removed is a giant lobster. For real. It's like red onesie pajamas, with an orange belly and a lobster-shaped hood with eyes the size of tennis balls. I clap both hands over my mouth in shock. Somehow this makes me feel triumphant, like the universe is siding with me in the Shellfish Holmes debate, and I shed my anger.

"What?!" I mumble-exclaim at the same time Izzy says, "*How?*"

Our laughter spurts out like shaken soda cans spraying around the room, and it's the old Izzy and Maizy again. The release feels so good, and our argument over a school project seems ridiculous. Even more ridiculous than this lobster costume.

"It's fate!" Izzy wheezes, wiping tears from her eyes.

I can't stand straight, I'm laughing so hard, but I nod in agreement.

"We don't have to use Lois," Izzy says. "*You* can be Shellfish Holmes! You have to wear this. You have to!"

"I do," I agree. "I totally do!"

Still giggling, I reach down to the book box, but it's empty now except for a card. I pick it up and realize it's not a card—it's actually a photo. An old photo with a digital date stamped on the bottom: 4-16-1993.

There are three women smiling at the camera, and my gaze locks on one. I know that smile. I've known that smile my whole life. The wisp of a shiver tiptoes down my spine as I look from the photo to the empty box, trying to make sense of how it got there.

"What is it?" Izzy asks.

I turn the photo toward her and tap the woman on the right. "That's Jacuzzi."

2

Ice Cream Escape

"I think so."

A stranger eavesdropping would probably think Izzy's disbelief came from me stating that a person was a hot tub. But Izzy knows my grandma Susie, and she knows that when I was three, "Jacuzzi" was how I said her name, and it stuck. She's been our Jacuzzi ever since.

I study the picture some more. There's Jacuzzi, and another woman who looks about the same age, and in between them stands an older white-haired lady. All three have big smiles on their faces, and they're dressed up like they're at a special event, maybe a wedding or something like that.

"Jacuzzi kind of looks like your mom there," Izzy says.

I take in the pile of books on the table in front of me. "I wonder if she left these outside."

That would be a weird thing for Jacuzzi to do. Why wouldn't she just leave them on our front porch or give them to us in person?

"Hey, Mom!" I leave the storage room and find her in the front. The "Closed" sign has been flipped to "Open," and she's rearranging things in the window to make space for the frame. Once it's filled with marbles, the floor will be spotted with rainbows when the sun hits it in the afternoon.

I hold the photo out to her. "Look what I found in that box."

Mom leans close for a good look. "That's Jacuzzi," she says.

"I know!"

Mom's brow is folded up, like she's waiting for the punch line of a joke.

"It was in that box," I say again. "Along with all the books."

"That makes no sense," Mom says.

I shrug. I don't know what else to say.

Mom heads back to the storage room, and I follow her. When she sees all the books, she breathes in sharply. She lifts up one, then another. *The Secret at Shadow Ranch. The Haunted Bridge.*

"These are Nancy Drews!"

The name Nancy Drew rings a bell, but I didn't realize that's what those books were, or that the series was so old.

"Why did she do this?" Mom seems to be asking the books this question, more than me and Izzy.

She pulls out the basket where she stores her purse and retrieves her phone. A few taps on the screen, and she waits with it pressed to her ear. There's a faraway tinny voice of Jacuzzi, and my mom says, "Mom, what were you thinking?"

Izzy and I exchange a look, our eyes wide. Mom sounds…really annoyed…and I don't understand how a box of old books and a photo could rile her up.

"I don't mean for dinner tonight," Mom continues. "I mean the box you left outside the store. Nancy Drews—seriously? Is that supposed to be a joke? And you didn't drive those over here, did you?"

Now I think I might understand—at least a little bit. Jacuzzi injured her foot a few weeks ago, and her doctor still hasn't given her the okay to use her car.

Izzy mouths, *Ice cream?*

I may have been annoyed about her wanting to go to Scoops earlier, but now I'm relieved at the excuse to get away.

I tell Mom we'll be back, and she nods, but she's saying, "The books. The books, Mom. You left them outside the store!"

Once we're outdoors waiting to cross at the corner, Izzy says, "That was *so* awkward!"

"I don't understand what just happened."

"Why was your mom so mad about books?"

I shrug. The whole thing has me confused—why my grandmother would leave them outside the store like that, why it bothered Mom so much.

We walk past workers taking down the floral hanging baskets from the lampposts and replacing

them with scarecrows. I push open the door to the
ice cream shop, and Max calls, "Welcome to Scoops,"
before looking up. He flicks the hair out of his eyes
as he offers a cone to an elderly man holding a little
boy's hand. Then he spots us.

"Hey, Maize."

As we wait for Max to finish ringing up his customer, Izzy whispers, "You're so lucky."

"Why?"

"You can come here whenever you want."

I frown at Izzy, because she's never been that
into ice cream, but then I see she's watching the
back corner where the arcade games are. Just like
she thought, Link and Ben are there, laughing and
pounding their hands against the controls. I don't
have to be a brilliant detective to figure out it's not
the ice cream she wants to spend more time with.

When we step up to the counter, my brother says,
"Isabelle! What are you up to these days?"

I'd forgotten, again, that Isabelle is what she
wants to be called now. The funny thing is, Max has
always called her Isabelle. He started doing that in
the third grade, to tease her. That was when she

hated her full name. He has no idea how pleased it must make her now.

She straightens, and flips her hair over one shoulder. "I was working at Alter Ego, with Maizy." Her eyes flit back and forth from my brother to Ben and Link in the corner. They've shown zero sign of being aware of anything other than the game they're playing.

"Working, huh? Aren't you too young to have a job?" Max says.

She bats his question away with a swat of her hand. "Well, you know, *volunteering*."

Behind her, I can't help rolling my eyes, which my brother catches. But all he says is, "That's very charitable of you."

Max offers us samples, but Izzy says she's not in the mood for ice cream and wanders to the back.

I watch her go, and Max says to me, "You should have ice cream."

He doesn't wait for my reply and fills a cup with one scoop of rocky road and another of bubblegum.

"Have you seen Jacuzzi today?" I ask.

"This morning? No, I haven't. Aren't we having dinner at her house?"

That's our Saturday family routine. Sometimes it's dinner at her house, sometimes at ours, or sometimes we meet at a restaurant.

"Yeah, but she left something at the store, and Mom was weird about it. I thought maybe she stopped in to say hi to you."

Max shakes his head. "Haven't seen her. I wouldn't worry about it, though."

I didn't say anything about being worried, but I guess my face did.

I take my ice cream to the back. Link's twin sister, Cam, is there too, sitting in a booth with a book.

"Hi, Cam," I say. It must be a good book, because she doesn't look up.

"And it's hilarious," Izzy is saying. She waves me over. "Maizy, come here. I was telling them about your script for Mr. Orson's class. Tell them how funny it is."

I feel a little taller, hearing Izzy rave over something I wrote. But at the same time, I don't know if she really means it. Maybe she's just trying to impress the boys.

Link and Ben turn, eyebrows raised and waiting for me to crack them up, I guess.

"Umm…"

Ben is one of the shorter boys in our class, and he's very smiley. If he's not smiling, then he looks like he's trying not to. Link's face is just neutral. He tugs on the strings of his Larksville Soccer hoodie so they're sliding back and forth to the electronic beat of the home screen on the game they'd been playing.

Finally, I say, "It's…funny."

Ben goes, "Heh," like I actually told a joke, but he's nice like that. Link nods and says, "Okay." He turns back to the game and puts in another quarter.

"Ooh, I want a turn," Izzy says, and squeezes by Ben to claim the second controller. Ben leans against the machine to watch them play.

And I stand alone, behind them.

Cam turns a page, continuing to be absorbed in her book. My brother is on the far side of Scoops,

bringing extra napkins to the elderly man, whose grandson's cone dripped all over the table.

This is feeling super awkward, staring at the backs of Izzy, Link, and Ben. And I know from being here during the summer that Izzy's pretty good at this game, so I might be standing here for a while. I pull my phone from my pocket and look at the screen, pretending to see a message from my mom.

"Oh, hey, my mom needs me back at the store."

I wait, giving Izzy a chance to tell me to hold on, she's coming too. But she keeps playing.

"So, um, I should get going."

I might as well be a lamp for how interested she is in me.

"Okay, so…Gotta run."

I raise a hand, waggle my fingers, and say, "Toodles!"

Toodles? Where did that come from?

I spin away before Izzy or anyone else sees my face flame bright red. They're still into the game, but I hear Cam snort. I move like a person with places to go, who totally meant to say *toodles* (ugh), but then I push the wrong side of the door and it doesn't open.

"It's the other side, dear—" says the elderly man.

"THANKS," I reply, way too loud.

I'm finally outside the ice cream shop. I head for the crosswalk, completely embarrassed, but even more than that, I'm annoyed. Annoyed that Izzy pretended to want to help at my mom's store. Annoyed that she tried to use my funny script to impress Link and Ben. Annoyed that the only time she seemed to remember I existed was when she was telling them about it. And I'm annoyed that she treated me like a lamp.

But also? I acted like a lamp. So I'm annoyed at myself too.

Because nobody can treat you like a lamp if you act like a spotlight.

Bells jingle behind me as someone else leaves Scoops, and my spirits lift with the hope that it's Izzy, coming after me to apologize. I don't want to give her the satisfaction of an easy apology, so I stare straight ahead, but that resolve melts in seconds. I don't like playing dramatic games. I just want things to be normal with us. I turn, preparing to smile and brush off the whole morning, but it's not Izzy who walked out. It's Cam.

She's also wearing a Larksville Soccer sweat-shirt, like her brother, only hers is green instead of gray. Cam's hair is short like Link's, but she has magenta streaks in the dark curls on top of her head. She jogs up to me, then comes to a stop, feet spread apart and straddling a crack in the sidewalk. She jabs her hands into the front pocket of her hoodie and says, "So this funny movie of yours. Isabelle wants to meet at the park later to work on it. At three, if that works for you."

I feel like I'm trying to do a complicated math problem in my head. Is Cam telling me this because Izzy wants to work on the movie, just me and her like we'd planned? Or did she actually ask Link and Ben to join our group? Did they say yes? Is Cam part of the group project too?

"I...well, uh..."

Do the answers to my questions really matter? It's only a school project, and maybe a bigger group would be more fun, like Izzy said. And there are a lot of roles in the script, and if we're not going to use stuffed animals, then having more people would be easier than if Izzy and I played multiple parts.

"Sure, yeah, fine," I say, not entirely certain what I'm agreeing to.

Cam turns to jog back. "Cool," she says over her shoulder, clearing up absolutely nothing.

3

Old and Blue and Valuable Too?

"OH, GOOD, YOU'RE BACK," MOM SAYS WHEN I PUSH OPEN ALTER EGO'S front door. She's filling the frame with marbles, humming along to an old song called "I'm Still Standing" that's on one of her store mixes. My dad designed the frame so each narrow shelf pulls out; that way if a customer wants to buy a specific marble, it's easy to get to. Marvin sits beside Mom's feet, his tail swishing as he looks up at the frame. Every so often he stretches out a paw to bat at a marble through the glass.

I want to ask about the call with Jacuzzi, but I also *don't* want to at the same time. The fact that Mom is humming might make it seem as if everything ended well, but sometimes her humming can be like a cat's purring. Maybe the cat is happy, or maybe it's in distress and trying to soothe itself.

Mom juts her chin in my direction, and I notice that the dolly and the box of books have been wheeled next to the front door. "Can you take those down to Maureen?"

I stare at the box for a second, confused, because if it was Jacuzzi who left it, she definitely wouldn't have mixed up our store and Turn the Page.

"That was meant for the bookstore and not us?"

Mom shrugs. "All I know is I'm not selling them. Maybe Maureen will want them."

"You're giving them away? And Jacuzzi's okay with that?"

"Well, your grandmother claims they're not from her. So it doesn't matter if she's okay with it or not."

Uh-oh. Mom never calls Jacuzzi *your grandmother*.

I wheel the dolly and the books out of there, sing-ing, "'I'm still standing, better than I've ever been...'" Even though I'm confused about what's going on, I can't help it. It's a catchy song.

There are more people out on Main Street now than earlier. A yoga class must have just ended upstairs, because a herd of leggings-clad people crosses at the intersection with me. They enter the smoothie place, and I continue rolling the box of books down the street. I pass an older man asking one of the workers who is fastening a scarecrow to a lamppost what they plan to do with the old summer flower baskets. A sparkly teal cruiser bike, locked in the rack between the bank and Turn the Page, catches my eye. The door to the bookstore is propped open with a sign advertising upcoming events, so it's easy enough to bump the dolly over the threshold, but I'm looking at the bike and not where I'm going, and *BAM!* The dolly and cardboard box crash into the banned-books table display. Books topple to the floor.

Maureen and the customer she's helping at the counter both turn at the sound of my collision.

"Whoops! Sorry about that," I say as I pick up the fallen books.

"You need driver's ed to learn how to steer that thing, Maizy," Maureen calls.

"Sorry," I say once more, placing *Melissa* and *The Hate U Give* and *Speak* back on their stands. When the table display is fixed, I wheel the box behind the counter and set it next to Maureen.

The customer, a girl maybe a few years older than Max, is pulling book after book out of a messenger bag and setting them on the counter between us. The pile keeps growing, as if the messenger bag is a clown car for books.

"Store credit or cash this time, Kelsey?" Maureen asks.

"Depends." The girl adds the last title to her stack, then unfolds a piece of paper and smooths it on the counter, sliding it over to the side where Maureen and I stand. "Do you have any of these? They're for my classes."

She must go to Larksville College. Max didn't apply there because the tuition is too expensive without loans or scholarships. My parents have said we can go to any college we want, as long as the amount they've been saving since we were little is enough to cover it.

As Maureen starts typing into her computer, checking if she has the books on the list, Kelsey rummages through a bowl of mini erasers on the counter. Maureen glances at me over her orange-framed glasses.

"What's in the box, Maizy? Something for me, I take it?"

"Oh, umm…I guess? Someone left a bunch of books outside our store this morning. Mom doesn't want them, but she thought you might."

"I'm a little tight on shelf space for used books at the moment, but the library might like them for their fundraising sale coming up," Maureen says.

As Maureen and I talk, Kelsey scoops an eraser into her palm and places her hand on the counter in a loose fist, concealing what's inside. At least, I think I saw her scoop up an eraser. Her eyes are on Maureen, who is squinting at her computer, then Kelsey looks up to the ceiling, over to the bookcases—everywhere but the eraser bowl she was fascinated with seconds ago.

Did I just witness Kelsey *stealing* an eraser?

The bowl looks as full as it did before, but it's a mix of food-themed erasers, and it's not like I memorized the order they were piled in. I study Kelsey's hand, trying to see if there's anything hidden under her fingers, but I can't tell.

"Someone left you a whole box of books?" Kelsey's voice startles me from obsessively staring at her hand. Her face gives away nothing. She leans forward to look over the counter at the box between my feet and Maureen's. "Oooooh! Are those Nancy Drews?"

I look down to the books. "How did you know?"

"I'd recognize that silhouette anywhere. Could I see one?"

Kelsey holds out a hand, the one that would have held an eraser, but it's empty. Was it always empty, or did she move it when I looked away? Did she return the eraser to the bowl or put it in her pocket? I reluctantly bend down and retrieve a book from the box, passing it over to Kelsey.

"I loved Nancy Drew when I was a kid," Maureen says. "I always wanted to be like her. Driving around in her blue convertible, solving other people's problems. She could do anything! Made me feel like I could do anything too, if I put my mind to it." She glances around her store before returning to her keyboard.

"Like have my own bookstore, for example." Maureen peers at the screen and murmurs, "Living the dream."

"I'd love to have my own bookstore," Kelsey says. "I would read all day, arrange books…"

"Mmm-hmm…" Maureen marks a check next to a title on Kelsey's list.

I assume Maureen loves to read, but every time I'm in her store, she's busy doing other stuff.

"Oh, wow, look!" Kelsey turns the open book to face us. "Copyright 1930. That's almost a hundred years ago!"

"Really?" Maureen says. "Huh. I don't think the ones I read were quite that old."

"So, you don't want these?" Kelsey asks me. "One of my professors actually collects old series. She talked about Nancy Drew in my women's studies class and how she was a role model for a lot of women. If you're giving these away, I'll take them. Maybe my professor will want them, and if she doesn't, maybe I'll start my own collection."

"Well…"

Mom doesn't want the books, and I'd been planning to hand them over to Maureen, but there's something about Kelsey being so interested that makes me want to hold on to them. Or at least not give them to this maybe-an-eraser-stealing girl.

Maureen interjects. "Have you read any Nancy Drew, Maizy?"

I shake my head.

"You should hold on to those and read them. And make sure they're not valuable before you do anything else with them."

"They could be valuable?" I ask. "Because they're old?"

"Well, not because of age alone, but a lot of people collect Nancy Drew titles," Maureen clarifies. She marks another check next to a book on Kelsey's list. "A Nancy Drew specialist would be able to tell you if there's anything noteworthy about those."

"Here." Kelsey rips off a blank corner from the sheet of titles Maureen is checking and grabs a pen from the mug next to the register. She jots down her name and an email address and slides the paper over to me. "My professor might be a good person to talk to if you want to learn more about Nancy Drew. She's brilliant."

"Oh...okay." I tuck the paper inside the book to be polite and put it back in the box, but I can't imagine actually talking to this college professor. When we went to Max's senior awards banquet in the spring, two different teachers came by to talk to my parents about how much they loved having him as a student. I just sat there, smiling and blinking like a creepy doll. And those were high school teachers, so I don't see myself rolling this box into a college professor's office and chatting it up.

I wheel the dolly back to the entrance, being extra careful this time as I round the front display table.

Mom won't be thrilled to see the books return, so I use an extra-bright and chipper voice when I reenter Alter Ego. "They're back!" Hopefully that will defuse her irritation.

It doesn't.

"Don't tell me Nancy Drew is still in that box."

She said *Don't tell me*, so I don't say anything.

Mom tosses her hands toward the box like she can't deal with it anymore. "Take them to the back," she says, sounding defeated. "We'll bring them home and return them to Jacuzzi tonight."

Later that day, I'm passing time in my room until I meet Izzy at the park. Along with the box of books, the lobster costume came home with me. Mom let me borrow it for our class project, so it's tossed on my bed. I'm draped over my poufy chair, holding open one of the Nancy Drew books.

Since I didn't have the nerve to ask Mom why these books bothered her, I decided to try reading one, thinking maybe as soon as I started it, I'd go, "Ooooooooh, now I see what the problem is!"

But a few pages in, I still don't get it.

I also don't get how this book is supposed to be

a mystery. So far, the story is about Nancy picking flowers that are the same color blue as her eyes and she wants to win a prize for her bouquet and *yaaaaaaaawwwn*...What kind of an exciting mystery is that?

Then it hits me: flowers!

That's the solution to the problem with my movie script! Now we can move forward with filming, like Izzy has been wanting, and I won't have any reservations about the story not being quite finished. I'm so excited, I toss Nancy Drew aside and pick up my phone.

"I figured it out!" I text Izzy.

Then I stare at the screen.

After a minute, I add, "The murder! I know how it happens!"

Still no reply from Izzy. Maybe she's outside or watching TV with the volume really loud. She's probably not ignoring me.

It's almost time to go, anyway.

The lobster costume has one arm folded up, like it's waving, which makes me think: What if I wear it to the park? A smile pushes its way onto my face as

I imagine Izzy's reaction—first surprise, then hysterical laughter, like the way we laughed over the costume this morning.

I have to wear it to the park. It would be too funny not to.

I step into the costume, one fleece leg at a time, giggling as I zip up the front. Goodbye, Maizy Turner; hello, Shellfish Holmes.

The claws are separate pieces that strap to my wrists, which is good because I'll be able to grip my handlebars. I hoist my backpack onto my shoulders and leave through the back door.

My bike is leaning against the house. I strap on my helmet but then realize it's not the full lobster effect without the hood up.

Might as well go all in, I think, and slide it over the helmet.

I swing a fuzzy red leg over my bike, and soon I'm pedaling down the street with a lobster tail wagging over my back tire.

4

Lobster Surprise

IZZY AND I ALWAYS MEET ON THE SIDE OF LARKSVILLE PARK THAT borders the college campus. There's a spot we found maybe a year ago—a clearing in a grove of pine trees where nobody else seems to go. It's like our own clubhouse. So that's where I'm headed.

I can't wait to see the look on her face when I get there. Her reaction when she hears my fix for the plot hole in *Shellfish Holmes* will be even better! I imagine the conversation as I pedal:

> **MAIZY:** Get this, the murder weapon is going to be…flowers!

IZZY: Flowers? How can flowers be used
as a weapon?

MAIZY: A bouquet is delivered to
the starlet on opening night from a
mysterious admirer. What she doesn't
know is that the jealous castmate sent
them. Tucked in the middle is a flower
that kills you by its scent alone! The
starlet takes one whiff and drops dead.

IZZY [gasps audibly]: That's genius!
You're so clever! How did you ever come
up with such a smart—

HOOOOOONNNK!

My imaginary scene is rudely interrupted by a
station wagon whizzing past, bass booming. A teenage kid yells out the window, "Nice pinchers!"

My neck—which is already hot and damp from
the sun beating down on me—flares hotter. I'm so
startled and flustered, I don't even yell back to correct him that they're *pincers*.

I bow my head and keep pedaling through the
outskirts of campus. Apartment buildings and

townhomes blur on either side of me. There's a football game today, and every so often the cheers of the distant crowd drift over, even though the college stadium is several miles away. I pretend the cheers are the audience who will watch *Shellfish Holmes* when our project is picked to premiere at the Curio. I use that as motivation to get back into a theatrical zone. By the time I reach the traffic signal that separates me from the park, I'm in the mindset of Shellfish Holmes.

Waiting for the light to change, I spot Izzy on the grass by the lake. I guess we're not meeting at our usual place. And it looks like it's not just the two of us either, because Izzy's not alone.

I use my elbow to push the button at the crosswalk and squint, making out Link, Ben, and I'm pretty sure Cam too. So Izzy did invite them to be in our group. Okay, that's fine. I take a deep breath, feeling a bit like I'm waiting in the wings to go onstage.

Izzy flips her long hair over her shoulder and looks my way. I know she sees me, because her mouth literally drops open. This is it! Showtime!

Struggling to keep a straight face, I raise a hand and wave. The lobster claw—which is about four times as large as my head—sways back and forth.

Instead of doubling over in laughter, Izzy is frozen. Link and Ben and Cam look my way now too, and a line of cars have come to a stop at the red light.

My waving lobster claw slows down as I mentally zoom away from myself, like a camera pulling back to take in the scene.

Nobody appears to find this as hilarious as I thought they would.

The crosswalk sign beeps.

The line of cars wait for me to cross.

Everyone's eyes are locked on me. I imagine there are even people in the windows of the homes behind me peering through curtains at the ridiculous lobster bicyclist.

I close my eyes and visualize my obituary: *Maizy Turner, budding movie director and shellfish aficionado, dropped dead of embarrassment while dressed as a lobster. In lieu of flowers, please send lemon and butter.*

I push off from the curb and keep my head down. My thoughts form a panicky swirl as I try to figure the best way out of this. The key, I think, is to commit to my character. I didn't do this just for a laugh, I try to convince myself. I wore the costume for the sake of the movie. We are here to work, and this fuzzy, heavy, slightly-damp-from-my-sweat getup is proof of how serious I am about my art.

I am one with the lobster! I am Shellfish Holmes!

Sweat trickles onto my forehead, between my eyebrows. A drop is creeping down the side of my nose, but I am a lobster detective, and the moisture is making me nostalgic for my ocean home.

Okay, I can't stand it. I jerk a hand up to wipe away the drop, but instead I bat myself in the face with my gigantic claw. Even though it's made of foam, it startles me enough that I rear back on my bike, then shift my weight forward and clamp my hand on the handlebar, trying to right myself, but my lobster tail has lodged somewhere on the back tire. The next thing I know I'm tipping...

Lobster down.

My brain must have shrunk to the size of a lobster's, because I did nothing to stop my fall. I'm pretty sure I keeled straight over like a bowling pin.

I'm still lying there, a tangle of fleece and foam and bike, when I hear a lady from one of the waiting cars call to me, "Are you okay?"

"Yep," I reply.

She opens her driver's-side door and helps me stand up. I'm briefly grateful for this plush onesie because while my upper arm and knee took the brunt of the fall, it doesn't feel like I'm too scraped up.

Brushing gravel from my sleeve, the lady comments, "Your costume's seen better days."

I'm sweaty and shaky, but I need to get out of this street before the light turns green and cars start honking.

"It's rough out here for a lobster," I reply. I get back on my bike and keep my eyes on my pedaling feet, wobbling the rest of the way across the street.

"You're Shellfish Holmes. You're Shellfish Holmes," I mutter, trying to imagine away my humiliation. The costume might be a little battered now, but I can incorporate this into the story. Maybe the detective had a run-in with a mob boss—an eel they call Mr. Slick? An octopus nicknamed Seven Arms?

Cheering and claps draw my attention as I reach the park side of the street. Link and Ben are applauding, like I pulled off an epic trick that impressed them.

Izzy marches over, arms crossed and a scowl on her face, and I stop my bike at the edge of the grass. You'd think she'd at least be concerned about my fall, or sympathetic to the fact that I'm dressed in a lobster plushie on a hot September afternoon. The old Izzy would have run to me the second she saw me go down. She would have helped me get up, and we'd be laughing about the whole thing. This Izzy bends over my handlebars, her face close to mine. A wave of her mom's floral perfume nearly knocks me back to the ground.

"What is wrong with you?" she whispers. "Showing up here like this?"

She flaps a hand in front of my costume like she's the world's angriest game show hostess. Izzy says more words, but I'm distracted by this idea of a disgruntled game show hostess, and how it would be a really funny character for a skit or movie, especially if the game show was super bright and cheesy...

"Is this *funny* to you?" Izzy's voice pierces through.

"Yes," I say reflexively, before realizing she and I aren't on the same page. We're not even in the same script at the moment. I can't believe I'm the one dressed as a lobster—a banged-up lobster at that—and *she's* the one acting humiliated.

"You told me to wear the costume, Izzy. You said I should be Shellfish Holmes."

"I didn't mean wear it to the park! On your bike!" Her voice gets more urgent with every sentence. "What is wrong with you? When are you going to grow up, Maizy? We're sixth graders now. Act like it." She begins to walk back to our classmates but whirls around. "And how many times do I have to tell you? It's Isabelle."

Here's an interesting fact I learned when I wrote my script: Lobsters have teeth in their stomachs instead of in their mouths. And right now, my stomach feels like it's gnawing on rocks, which makes me wonder if maybe the costume has magical properties and I'm actually turning into a lobster, bit by anatomical bit.

Cam calls over, "Maizy, are you joining us?"

"No. She's not," Isabelle answers for me, her words sharp and crisp.

I'm pretty certain my entire body has flushed lobster red. I imagine antennae sprouting from my head, and the foam claws melding with my hands, and then with a *pop!* my whole body will condense into small lobster form and I can scurry off into the man-made lake, which I'd planned to use for the opening beach scene in our movie. My movie.

Instead, I push off and pedal myself in a U-turn to head back home, my bent lobster tail drooping behind me.

Sunbeams push through the arched branches of trees lining my street, baking me in this costume. I wish there was a breeze. I can't wait to get inside and peel off this lobster and forget I ever even dreamed up this dumb detective.

If I wasn't already uncomfortable enough, I spot my next-door neighbor Nell crossing the lawn with her mom. The Kapadias live in a two-story house that always looks like it's basking in the sunshine. Nell's yard has an actual picket fence—it's that kind of perfect home. My house is much smaller and hunkers under an oak tree that is decades older than our neighborhood.

Nell is wearing a hat that I'm sure she decorated herself with handmade fabric flowers—she's super crafty and the only person in our entire school who could pull off that look. Or, at least, the only person *willing* to pull off that look. When we were little, we were best friends. Our friendship was pretty much inevitable, since we live next door to each other and are the same age. That's why I know so many things about her, like her favorite color is orange, she sleeps with a fuzzy hippo named Bubba, she takes a trip to India every other summer to visit her dad's family, she had nightmares after we watched this old movie called *The Princess Bride*, and she hates it when people think she's adopted because her mom has pale skin and dirty-blond hair.

Nell and I were inseparable until third grade, when we were placed in different classes. Nell started a sewing club and wanted me to join, but I began writing movie scripts with Izzy at recess. I thought making movies was more fun, Nell thought making clothes was more fun, and we just kind of went our separate ways.

The Kapadias' station wagon chirps as it's unlocked, but Nell's mom doesn't open the door. Instead, she shades her eyes and looks my way. I hear her say, "What in the world...," as my bike squeaks closer.

I coast by and duck my head in a futile attempt to conceal myself, but Nell calls out, "Hey, Maizy!"

My hand reacts like it's preprogrammed to wave and I raise a claw, but my bike wobbles and I clamp my fingers back around the handlebars. "Hi, Nell. Hi, Mrs. Kapadia," I call back.

"Looking good! Love the costume!" Nell smiles and hops in the back seat of their car, as if it's not at all weird to see me ride past her house dressed as a lobster, but her mom can't stop staring as I coast into my driveway.

A miniature *Isabelle* perches on my shoulder and hisses in my ear, *When are you going to grow up, Maizy?* Instead of making me want to grow up, remembering her words makes me want to rewind time and go back to being even younger. Back to when Nell asked me to join her sewing club. But this time I'd say yes.

I push my bike up the drive and nudge our side gate open with my front tire. When I walk through, a lobster appendage snags on the fence. One spindly little arm tugs and tugs, trying to hold me back as I lunge forward to break free. Finally, I hear a rip, and I'm wheeling my bike down the path once again, too exhausted by the drama of this afternoon to care what exactly tore.

As soon as I'm inside, I unzip the lobster suit. The top half flops from my shoulders to the floor and brings the legs down with it, like it's as relieved to not be worn as I am to not wear it. I high-step out of the costume, wearing only the shorts and

T-shirt I had on underneath, and leave it piled behind me.

Entering my room, I nearly trip over the Nancy Drew book I tossed aside earlier. I pick it up and sigh, remembering my poisonous flower as a weapon. I never got to tell Izzy about that. I still really like the idea.

On the cover of the old book, Nancy Drew's dark blue silhouette bends toward the title with her magnifying glass, like she's investigating the words *The Password to Larkspur Lane*. There's an illustration on the first page of a teenage girl—Nancy, I assume—hiding in shrubs, with a spooky-looking man shining a flashlight her way. This doesn't look like a boring story about a girl picking flowers. I flip to where I left off and skim the rest of the page. It turns out, things take a dramatic turn in a matter of sentences: Nancy's flower picking is interrupted by a plane that's about to crash, which hits a pigeon that Nancy rescues, and then she discovers it's a carrier pigeon with a coded message tied to its foot.

And I thought my mystery was over-the-top.

I drop into my poufy chair and keep reading.

Before I know it, Mom is calling my name from downstairs and nearly an hour has passed. If I'd only read one more paragraph earlier today, I might have gotten sucked into this book, forgotten to meet Izzy, and avoided the whole lobster debacle.

Mom appears in my doorway, holding the saggy exoskeleton of Shellfish Holmes. "Why did you leave this on the floor? And…" She scans the costume up and down. "What *happened* to it?"

I was so ready to shed my lobster shell, I never really looked it over. Boy, does it look bad. Grimy and torn, like it had a tussle with a sea lion.

"How am I supposed to rent this at Alter Ego, Maizy? It's ruined. This was our only lobster costume."

I want to say, *Is there* really *a demand for lobster costumes?* But I know better.

Mom continues. "Somebody put a lot of hard work into making this and had it on consignment. You know what that means, right?"

As if I didn't feel bad enough, it hadn't occurred to me that ruining the costume meant whoever made it wouldn't be able to rent it out anymore. I stare at the pages of my book, wishing I could hop inside Nancy's roadster and zoom off with her. "Yes, I know."

"How did this happen, anyway? You only brought it home from Alter Ego a few hours ago!"

"I fell riding my bike."

I'm still staring at the book, but I hear the fabric brush the floor as Mom lowers the costume and the tension leaves her voice.

"Oh, Maize. Are you okay?"

"Yeah. Because of the lobster. It took most of the damage."

"You were...wearing this? While riding your bike?"

Mom presses her lips together, and I can tell she's trying not to laugh. I have to admit, the visual *is* funny.

"Do I even want to know why?"

"It was for a school project."

"Oh, sure, that makes perfect sense," she says, but shakes her head like *No it doesn't*.

I bite back a smile.

"I'm glad you're not hurt, Maizy, but you do need to make this right."

"I know," I say. "I'll pay for it."

I have no idea how much a lobster costume costs, but hopefully the $43 I have tucked inside my hollowed-out *Little Women* will cover it. I was saving up for a fancy audio recorder, but I guess improved sound quality in my movies will have to wait.

"And write an apology too. I'll look up who's consigning this costume and get you their name."

5

Spadle-Spoodle-Scoodle-Snowdle

THAT EVENING MY FAMILY IS IN THE CAR, HEADED TO JACUZZI'S, THE box of Nancy Drew books squeezed between me and Max in the back seat. We're returning the books to Jacuzzi, but I hold *The Password to Larkspur Lane* in my hands. I'm almost done and want to find out how it ends. On top of the box is a prototype for one of my dad's latest inventions, called the Spadle. Or maybe it's Spoodle? I can't remember, but it's supposed to be a cooking spoon, ladle, and spoon rest all in one. He's taking it to Jacuzzi to test out.

None of my dad's inventions have been successful yet, but that doesn't keep him from trying. He spends almost all his free time in a shed in our backyard dreaming up new ideas for something that will make us enough money that he can quit his soul-sucking job at a software company. (His words, not mine.)

I open my book to read, and Max glances over.

"That's one of these books?" He taps the box with his fingers. I nod and show the cover.

"Jacuzzi will love that you're reading Nancy Drew," Mom says. "She was always trying to get me to read those when I was your age."

The way she says this makes me imagine Jacuzzi bugging her to read Nancy Drew the way Mom bugs me to brush my teeth.

"Is that why it bothered you that she left them? Did you think she was telling you again to read them?"

Mom laughs. "When you say it out loud, it sounds a bit ridiculous, but it probably wouldn't have gotten under my skin the same way if it had been any other collection of books. Mainly, though, I was worried about how she got that box to the store with her fractured foot."

"Maybe someone else drove her," Dad suggests.

"That could be true," Mom says.

"Well, I like this one so far." I recount what's happened, finishing with, "So now the carrier pigeon that Nancy suspects is part of a crime ring was accidentally released and she's chasing it in her roadster."

"Too bad she doesn't have the Spoodle," Max says, picking up the prototype. "She could use it to launch a net and trap the bird." He presses an imaginary button, like he's ejecting a net.

"Spadle!" Dad corrects from the front seat. Then he lifts a finger. "Oh! Max, maybe the Spadle could also work as an ice cream scoop! Four uses in one, imagine that."

"You might need to change the name, then," Mom says.

"Scoodle?" I suggest.

"I don't know," Max says. "I'm not sure the ice

cream scoop needs improvement. Maybe the Spadle could be a snowball launcher?" He mimics digging and pitching something across the car.

"The Snowdle?" Mom says.

We continue to debate names and potential uses until we park in front of Jacuzzi's home. She lives in a small yellow house down the street from the Larksville Library.

Jacuzzi comes out to greet us right away, like she's been waiting at the window. Today she looks like a giant slice of watermelon—literally, her dress is magenta with black dots and a green band of fabric around the bottom. She always says she's too old not to have fun with how she dresses. It looks like she's wearing a snow boot on one foot and a sandal on the other, but this isn't part of her dressing-for-fun. The "snow boot" is actually a walking boot for her fractured foot.

"You don't have to come out to greet us," my mom says. "You should have your foot up and resting."

Jacuzzi swats her words away. "Don't be silly! It barely hurts anymore."

"You should at least use your crutches," Mom says.

"To walk halfway down my front path?" Jacuzzi wraps me in a hug. "I'm fine. Moving around is good for me."

Max is holding the box of Nancy Drews, so Jacuzzi gives him a sideways hug and says, "What's in there?"

"We're returning your books," Mom replies.

Jacuzzi sighs. "Not that again—"

Dad swings his prototype in between Mom and Jacuzzi, like a referee with a whistle, and practically sings, "We brought you this!"

She accepts it, probably grateful for the change in subject. "Is it a back scratcher?"

Dad cringes. "No! No, no. It's a combination cooking spoon, ladle, and spoon rest."

Jacuzzi assesses the Spadle, turning it this way and that. "Can it dish up pie? Because I made a certain college student's favorite."

"Pumpkin?" Max perks up. "Thanks, Jacuzzi."

Our grandmother points the Spadle-Spoodle to the house and marches up her path, like she's leading a parade. "To the pie!"

Mom trails behind her. "Before dinner? Seriously?"

"What's the difference if it goes before or after the chicken? Pumpkin's a vegetable anyway, isn't it?"

We file inside and kick off our shoes.

"I think it's fruit," I say. "It has seeds and grows from a flower, right?"

"Even better, then!"

Max sets down the box, and we gather around the kitchen peninsula, where Jacuzzi serves us pie. She uses the Spadle-Spoodle, which ends up making the slices look more like sloppy scoops.

"Well, thanks for trying," Dad says, accepting his plate. "I'll cross pie server off the list of potential uses."

Max takes a bite. "Still warm," he says.

Mom must have forgotten her no-dessert-before-dinner rule, because she accepts a plate too. For a few minutes, the kitchen is filled with jazz and the sound of us eating.

Propped up next to Jacuzzi's stove is a small painting I don't recognize.

"Is that new?" I ask between bites of pie.

"Yes! I made it a few days ago at my neighbor's painting party."

It's a painting of a bicycle with a flower-filled basket. Mom reads the words that wrap around the perimeter: "'Life is like riding a bicycle. You don't fall unless you stop pedaling.'"

"Or you're wearing a lobster costume," I add.

Dad and Max look confused. Jacuzzi probably is too, but she raises her eyebrows and says, "That's true, I guess!"

But Mom laughs, and before I know it, I'm recounting the whole lobster incident for my family. There's something about turning an embarrassing moment into a scene that could be from a funny movie that makes my terrible afternoon feel a little less terrible.

When I repeat, *It's rough out here for a lobster*, Jacuzzi lets out the hooting laugh she does when something takes her by surprise. She squeezes my arm and says, "Oh, Maizy! You never cease to delight me."

We're scraping up last bites of pie from our

plates when Mom clears her throat. "About those books…"

Everybody quiets, even the jazz mellows, and for a minute there's nothing but awkward coughs and shifting feet.

"I should check on that squirrel-proof bird feeder out back," Dad says. "You want to come, Max? Maizy?"

I hold up my book. "I think I'll finish this."

I do want to finish the book, but to be totally honest, I want to hear the conversation between Jacuzzi and Mom.

"I'll go," Max says, slopping another piece of pie onto his plate before he follows Dad to the sliding glass door.

"Save room for dinner!" Mom calls after him.

"Don't worry, I've got a big appetite," he says.

Dad slides the door closed behind them, and Jacuzzi says to Mom, "If you're not going to take my word for it, then follow me."

I want to follow as well, but I said I was going to read, so I linger at the counter until Jacuzzi adds,

"If you're enjoying that book, Maizy, you might like to see this too."

She leads us into her guest room and gestures to one of the bookcases. "See? All my Nancy Drews are right here."

I've never paid much attention to the books in this room, but now I see the silhouette of a lady with a magnifying glass on two shelves full of books.

"Fifty-six titles, all accounted for," she adds.

"But..." Mom scans the shelves, shaking her head like she can't believe what she's seeing. "So you really didn't leave the box?"

"Of course not," Jacuzzi says.

Mom's shoulders relax. "I'm glad you weren't driving." She looks over the shelves one more time. "It still doesn't make sense, though."

I know what Mom is hung up on. She's probably thinking the same thing I am—what about the photo?

I run back to the box in the other room and retrieve it.

"This is why we thought the books belonged to you," I explain when I return. "It was in the box."

Jacuzzi bends forward, and I can tell from the way her eyes widen that she recognizes the photo. But then she purses her lips and squints, acting like it's some mysterious artifact she's studying. "I'm not sure I understand," she finally says. "What does that have to do with me?"

Mom tips her head back and groans. "Mom. *Really?* You don't recognize yourself?"

Jacuzzi's eyes widen again, but this time it's much more theatrical. Like Izzy reciting lines from one of our screenplays. "Me? Are you sure?"

She studies the image again. In it Jacuzzi—or the woman who looks like her—has long hair, and my grandmother's is now short and spiky and gray. She's plumper in the photo, but the smile and shape of her face and eyes are so Jacuzzi. I suppose it's possible it's someone else, but it really looks like her.

"Do you recognize the other people?" I ask. "Or the event?"

"Nothing is ringing a bell." Jacuzzi speaks slowly as she considers this. "But that was quite some time

ago." To Mom she says, "I mean, you don't remember everything you did thirty years ago, do you?"

"Well, I remember I was sixteen and you and Dad divorced." Mom states this simply, almost cheerily, like she's just stating facts, but Jacuzzi sags in response.

"Of course. You don't forget something like that."

Mom puts a hand on Jacuzzi's shoulder. "Sorry, Mom. That was a bad attempt at humor. Thirty years was a long time ago, like you said."

This might be an odd thing to admit, but it's hard to think of my grandmother being married, or even Mom having a dad. I mean, I can imagine it, but it's like a story I'm making up for myself. I never knew my grandfather. He died before I was born. And I don't think Mom was very close to him after her parents divorced, so even Max barely knew him. It's always been just Jacuzzi. I've never thought of her as part of a pair, unless the pair was Mom and Jacuzzi.

"Anyway, I don't sell books in the store," Mom says. "Do you want more Nancy Drews for your collection? Or I can donate them."

Words pop out of my mouth, surprising me: "I'll take them."

Jacuzzi lights up. "You want them?"

"The one I'm reading is pretty good. I'd like to read more."

There's something about all the twists and turns in Nancy's story that has me hooked. No matter what happens, Nancy can handle it.

Injured pigeon falls at your feet? Nancy takes care of it.

Sinister man who might abduct you? Nancy knows what to do.

But there's something else pulling at me to keep the books. Why did they show up at Mom's store? And why was a photo of my grandmother with them? What are the chances it's all a big coincidence? There must be an explanation, and it bothers me that we don't understand yet.

"Oh, that's wonderful!" Jacuzzi says, her eyes a little misty. "I always wanted your mother to read them, but she was only ever interested in those Sugar Valley High books."

"*Sweet* Valley, Mom. And they weren't the only books I read—not that there was anything wrong with them."

They leave the room bickering, but I'm still staring at the photo. I can't tell whether Jacuzzi really doesn't remember or she's pretending, but I believe her when she says she didn't leave the books.

But if Jacuzzi didn't leave the books, then who did? And why?

6

A New Clue

SUNDAY MORNING, I PICK UP *THE PASSWORD TO LARKSPUR LANE* FIRST
thing when I wake up. I was going to finish the book
last night, but then Nancy and her friend Helen were
preparing to sneak onto this property where these
crooks are holding a wealthy older woman captive.
The whole thing felt too creepy to read before bed,
so I put the book down and went to sleep.

And, boy, am I glad I did, because Nancy is soon
trapped and locked in a cistern, which is like a dark
and slimy hole in the ground. I might be sitting cross-
legged on my bed, but I'm also in another world,

stuck in that hole with Nancy and wondering how to get out.

A short time later I close the book, feeling like I've returned from an adventure. Nancy saves herself by escaping into a pigeon coop, then uses pigeons to send messages for help, and the bad guys are caught in the end because of her ingenuity. I flop back onto my pillow, and the spooky property and pigeon coop fade away and my hammock of stuffed animals and my sticker-covered closet door come back into focus.

No wonder Jacuzzi loves these books.

I return *Password* to the box of other Nancy Drews and go through the titles to decide which one to read next. *The Message in the Hollow Oak, The Clue in the Diary*...I settle on *The Haunted Bridge*, because I like the title.

"Knock, knock," Mom says from my doorway. "I looked up the owner of the lobster costume, and you might be surprised by who it is." She has a weird look on her face, like she can't wait to tell me.

"Is it...someone famous?" Not that there's anyone famous in Larksville, but I can't think of why else the person would matter.

Mom laughs. "No, no—they're not famous." Then, like she can't keep it inside any longer, she blurts, "It's Nell!"

I frown. "Nell? Nell Kapadia?"

"Yes!"

"But…"

Nell saw me yesterday is what I'm thinking. And all she said was hi. At least I think that's all she said—I can't remember her exact words now. But she definitely didn't say: *Hi, Maizy, and by the way, I made that lobster costume, and why is it all banged up?*

Mom must sense my confusion because she says, "I've told you before that she sewed several of the costumes we rent, haven't I?"

"Yes, you have." At least a dozen times. Mom really likes Nell. Back when the two of us first drifted apart, she was always suggesting doing something with Nell if I was bored. Eventually she stopped making those suggestions, but every so often she reminisces about a funny or sweet thing we did together.

"It's just that, if it's Nell," I explain, "then she

already saw me in the costume after I fell. And it didn't seem to bother her."

I'm hoping Mom will let the whole thing go now, but she only stares at me.

"So, she already knows that I wore it and it's damaged and…" My words trail off as Mom continues to stare, no longer looking delighted and amused.

"And I guess I still need to make it right."

Mom nods. "Yes, you do. Just as you would no matter who was consigning the costume for the store. Nell worked hard to make that, and we won't be able to rent it any longer. She deserves an explanation."

I sigh. There's no use arguing with my mom, and she's right, anyway. "Okay," I say. "I'll talk to her soon."

I was thinking later this week at school, maybe, but Mom says, "You should do it now. Then it's taken care of."

We compromise with me showering and eating a bowl of cereal first, but soon I'm standing on the Kapadias' front porch, ringing the doorbell. They used to have a little dog named Biscuit who yapped and yapped when I rang the bell, but Biscuit died of old age when we were in second grade. Nell and I spent a week writing odes to Biscuit. I wonder if she still has those saved somewhere.

Nell answers the door. If she's surprised to see me, she doesn't show it. She just smiles and says, "Hey, Maizy! How's it going?"

"Good. Um. So..." It feels weird to make small talk, so I launch right in. "About the lobster costume yesterday—my mom told me you made it for her store to rent?"

"Yes! What did you think? It wasn't itchy, was it? I tried to make it like comfy onesie pajamas."

"Um..." My memories are drenched in humiliation and regret, so it's hard to remember how the costume felt before all that. "It was really comfortable. The thing is—"

"Why were you wearing it, anyway?" Nell steps outside and closes the door behind her. She sits on her front step and tips her head toward the space next to her, like she's expecting me to sit too, so I do.

"It was for Mr. Orson's project. I wrote a screenplay called *Shellfish Holmes* about this lobster detective, and Izzy and I were helping my mom at her store and found the costume."

I glance down at the mention of Izzy. I'm not sure why it feels a little awkward to say her name. It's been years since Nell and I have hung out, and it's not like she doesn't know that Izzy and I are best friends. Plus, Nell gets along with everyone and has lots of friends. I mainly have…Izzy.

But when I look up, Nell isn't bothered at all by my bringing Izzy up. In fact, she seems delighted. "The costume was your fate!"

I can't help smiling with her. "That's what we thought!"

I explain how I wore the costume to film scenes at the park and how it got caught on my bike when I crossed the street and I fell. I leave out the part about Izzy getting mad.

"Maizy!" Nell cringes on my behalf.

"It was *so* embarrassing," I confess, but we're laughing together about it.

"I had no idea," Nell says. "You rode by yesterday like, *Hey, people, just another day on my bike in a lobster costume!*"

"Oh yeah, that was exactly what was going through my head." I pick a leaf off the shrub next to me. "The thing is, I totally wrecked your costume. I'm really sorry."

"Is that why you're here?" Nell bumps her shoulder to mine. "I honestly forgot I made that one, until I saw you yesterday. It's fun to make costumes. I just do it for practice. If someone rents one and I make a little money, that's a bonus.

"I do feel bad for you, though," Nell adds. "And your project."

What does she mean by that? Has Izzy been telling people about what happened at the park? Does Nell know something I don't? I look at her, a little wary.

"How are you going to be a lobster detective if the costume is ruined?" she explains.

"Oh!" I relax, relieved that's what she meant. "I don't know. I guess we'll figure something out."

"I might be able to fix it. Want me to take a look?"

"Well…sure," I reply.

Sometimes Nell's constant cheeriness can be irritating in that "too perfect" way, but right now I'm appreciating it a lot.

We cross her yard, then mine. "So, what are you doing for Mr. Orson's project?" I ask.

"I'm doing a one-woman fashion show," she says. "It's going to be epic."

"You're doing it by yourself?" I ask.

"Yep," Nell says.

On the outside, I act like this doesn't surprise me, but on the inside I'm kind of stunned. Mr. Orson let us decide how to organize ourselves for this project, and I hadn't paid attention to anything beyond me and Izzy being partners. Nell doesn't seem bothered by the fact that she's on her own, but I would be. I mean, I don't think I'd mind standing on a stage to introduce a movie I made, but I'd worry about what our classmates would think if I wasn't in a group or with a partner. Which doesn't really make sense, I guess, because I'm not judging Nell. Or if I am, I'm judging her in a positive way, because I *wish* I was brave enough to do something like that on my own.

Once inside my house, I call, "Nell's here!"

We head for the stairs, stepping around plastic tubs and bags gathered in our entry.

"What's all this?" Nell asks.

"Max is leaving for college this week," I explain.

We stop for a second and stare at the collection of stuff as if it's an exhibit in a museum. Funny how I haven't paid much attention to it until Nell said something, I guess because the pile appeared gradually over the past couple of weeks as Max packed, adding a box one day, a bag on another.

And then Nell and I walk up the stairs to my room, just as we've done a thousand times before, only many years ago.

I open my closet door to pull out the lobster costume, but Nell stops at my bulletin board. It's plastered with photos, mostly of me and Izzy. If I knew Nell would be coming over, I might have replaced some so it didn't seem like I was trying to rub the friendship in her face. There *is* one old photo of me and Nell when we were seven. She picks it out right away.

"Aww, I remember that summer! I cried and cried because I had to go to India but wanted to stay here. We made that paper doll together, right? What did we call her? It was something funny, like Pineapple."

"Piña Colada," I remind her. "After that song my mom liked, remember? And we cut the doll in half so she could be with both of us, even when we were far apart."

Nell giggles. "Yes! We were so weird!"

In the photo, Piña Colada is still in one piece. Our fingers each grip one of her flat hands, and our smiles are wide, with missing teeth.

I hand Nell the lobster costume. After holding it up and turning it this way and that, then laying it on my bed to look more closely at the rips and grime, she declares, "I can definitely salvage this. I could even customize it for your movie, if you want."

"Customize it?"

Nell lifts up one of the wide soft legs. "I could turn the legs into a skirt if you want Shellfish Holmes to be more feminine. Or I could add glasses—stuff like that."

I stare at the legs for an extra-long time because I'm surprised by the idea that Shellfish Holmes might wear a dress, and I'm surprised that I'm surprised. The thought of a lobster as a detective came to me so easily, but why didn't I imagine the detective as anything other than male? I mean, the original Sherlock Holmes was a guy, of course, and it seems like a lot of famous detective characters are guys. So I guess that's what I was thinking, but really, I *wasn't* thinking at all. I was following what had been done before. Shellfish Holmes was my own creation. I could imagine it however I wanted. And girls are famous detectives too—just ask Nancy Drew! Actually, Nancy would probably be really humble about it if you asked her, but her friends and family would be quick to talk her up.

I wish I could call Izzy and ask her what she thinks about making Shellfish Holmes a girl. I mean, I know I *could* call her, but…I'm not even sure if Izzy wants to do the project with me anymore. My stomach gets queasy thinking about these things. Not doing the project with Izzy feels like it means something more significant than simply not doing a project together.

"I'll check with Izzy and get back to you," I finally say.

Then Nell spots the box of Nancy Drew books between us on the floor.

"What are these?" She reaches into the box of books, then gasps. "Are these Nancy Drews?!"

"I got them yesterday. I've only read one so far, but it was pretty good."

"I have old ones too, but mine look different. They have yellow spines and pictures on the front. Where did these come from?"

"Jacuzzi—well, we thought they did, but I guess we don't know. Someone left the box outside my mom's store."

Nell looks up from the books, her eyes bright. "Very mysterious!"

"If you think that's mysterious, look at this." I grab the photo from my desk and kneel next to Nell to show her. "It was in the box with the books."

Nell takes one look at the photo and says, "That's Jacuzzi!"

"Exactly!" I say. "Mom and I recognized her right away—that's why we assumed she left the books. But then Jacuzzi said she didn't, and when we showed her the photo, she couldn't remember anything about it."

Nells eyes widen. "Is she…healthy?" She taps her temple and adds, "You know, mentally?"

I'm reminded that Nell's grandfather had Alzheimer's, and I'm sure that's what she's thinking about. "Yeah. I mean, as far as I know."

I scrutinize the photo for the millionth time, hoping to spot an important detail, like Nancy would. Some clue that would explain why the books showed up at our store or why Jacuzzi pretended not to recognize herself. But she and the two women standing next to her look like normal people from a long time ago. The background is a boring could-be-anywhere room. The only thing that stands out is the date printed on the bottom in glowing blue numbers like a microwave clock.

I underline the date with my fingertip.

"Have you looked that up?" Nell asks.

Why didn't I think of that before? Nancy Drew didn't have a computer or the internet, but if she did, I bet looking up the date would have been the first thing she would do after finding the photo. I grab my phone and search for April 16, 1993. I read out loud what I find:

"'Bill Clinton was the president of the United

States; a guilty verdict was reached in a case against police officers who beat a man named Rodney King; Chance the Rapper was born..."

Nothing related to the photo. I add Jacuzzi's name, "Susie Anderson" and "Susan Anderson," to my search, but only find the same information as before. Well, at least I feel a little better about not thinking to do that right away.

Nell continues to sift through the books. She flips through one, and a pressed flower floats from the pages.

"How pretty!" She holds it up between her fingers. "It's like a little hidden treasure."

This gives me another idea, something else I'm sure Nancy would have done immediately. I pick up a book and start looking through it, page by page.

"Let's see if we find anything else," I say.

We search carefully. I'm hoping we'll come across maybe a letter or postcard, but there's nothing in the first one I pick up, or the second. Nell doesn't find anything in hers either. I grab *The Message in the Hollow Oak* next. The book naturally opens to the title page, so I almost miss it, but when I flip back to see the pages I skipped, there's a message written in large, looping handwriting:

> *Friendship is no big thing.*
> *It's a million little things.*
>
> *Dear Annette,*
> *Thank you for a million little things.*
> *Happy 10th birthday!*
> *Your friend, Susie*
> *1959*

My mouth drops open. An inscription! An honest-to-goodness inscription. In *The Password to Lark-spur Lane*, an inscription on a bracelet was a big clue that helped Nancy solve her case.

"Look!" I show Nell. "And it's from *Susie*. As in my grandma Susie? Do you think they could be the same?"

Nell grins. "I think you've found your first mystery, Maizy Drew."

7

Holmes. Shellfish Holmes.

AFTER NELL LEAVES, I CAN'T STOP THINKING ABOUT THE INSCRIPTION in *The Message in the Hollow Oak*. Could the Susie who wrote in the book really be my Jacuzzi? I do the math and calculate that she would have been ten if she wrote it. Was that message from my ten-year-old grandmother to her best friend?

And the quote she wrote, about friendship being a million little things. That's so true! It's hard to sum up why I like (liked?) being friends with Izzy. The answer really would be a lot of little things strung together. She does these funny voices for her characters in our movies, and that always makes me laugh. And she stayed after school to help me look for my favorite sweater when I lost it. And she runs the mile next to me in PE, even though she could run much faster if she wanted to.

I wonder what some of the little things were for Susie and Annette. And who is Annette, anyway? Is she the person who left the box outside Alter Ego? Did all the books in the box belong to her, or just this one? Is she one of the women in the photo? I'm trying to remember if the photo had originally been tucked inside this book or a different one, or if it was just loose in the cardboard box. That seems like a useful thing to know, but I didn't pay attention when I found it. Nancy Drew would never have overlooked a detail like that!

Most Sunday afternoons Izzy and I meet at the park, but after what happened yesterday, I wasn't planning to go. We haven't talked since the lobster incident, but now this inscription has me thinking about our friendship. Maybe she hasn't called because she's feeling so bad about how she talked to me. Maybe she'll be there, ready to apologize.

Maybe she has an explanation for acting the way she did.

I open *The Message in the Hollow Oak* to the inscription one more time. Then I slide the book into my backpack and tell my parents I'm going for a bike ride. I could send Izzy a message to check if she wants to meet first, but something is pulling me to just go.

When I pedal up to the cluster of pines, I've nearly convinced myself she'll be there. I wheel my bike between the bristly branches of two trees and step into the clearing.

It's empty.

I rest my bike on the ground, pull the Nancy Drew book out of my backpack, and sit on the boulder. I'll read for a little bit, and maybe Izzy will show up.

But after five chapters, I'm still alone, so I get up and pedal back home.

For the rest of the weekend, I try to forget about Izzy, but as soon as I enter the school building Monday morning, she's all I can think about. My backpack feels like someone dropped a brick in it as I move through the hallway.

Who am I going to hang out with at recess and sit with at lunch if Izzy and I aren't talking? Is she going to ignore me today? Or embarrass me again in front of other people? How are we going to work together on the *Shellfish Holmes* movie for Mr. Orson's class if we aren't talking? Will we still work together? All these questions crowd around me in the hallway, and my stomach is starting to ache.

I round the corner to the south entrance bench, which is where Izzy and I always meet at the start of school, and I'm expecting it to be empty like our meeting spot at the park. But there's Izzy sitting on the bench. Just like normal.

I stop so suddenly, someone bumps me from behind. They keep walking, but I stand still, braced for...I don't know what. More of Izzy flipping her hair and snapping at me, *When are you going to grow up?*

But she doesn't do any of that. Instead, it's like every other Monday, with Izzy smiling widely.

"Maizy Daisy!" she calls, and gallops over. She stops with a half twirl in front of me, her blue skirt flaring out. "What do you think? Mom took me shopping yesterday."

"I think...cute?" My head is muddled. I was expecting everything to be different, but instead it's exactly the same. Am I dreaming? Or was it the lobster episode that was the dream?

Izzy's smile falls. "You don't like it, do you?"

I shake my head quickly. "No, no—I do! The skirt is really cute. I'm just...tired."

"Ahhh..." Izzy nods deeply, sympathetically. "A case of the Mondays."

The first bell rings, and Izzy links her arm through mine. We walk to Mr. Orson's class, just like always, and all those questions that slowed me down when I entered the school are left gathered behind us, scratching their heads and wondering what happened as they watch us walk away.

Mr. Orson takes attendance, and I go through the motions I always do—take out my notebook, take out a pen, flip to a clean page—but it feels like

I'm performing the role of myself on a typical Monday morning.

Everyone else is performing their roles too: Link's and Ben's desks are behind mine, and they're deep in discussion about a video game—very typical. Cam is a few desks away, concentrating on a book: also typical.

I keep glancing at Izzy, trying to catch some evidence of...I don't know what, exactly. What I *do* know is that, as relieved as I was when Izzy acted totally normal when I first saw her, it also feels uncomfortable to pretend Saturday afternoon didn't happen. Then I remember what I wanted to show her. I unzip my backpack, pull out the Nancy Drew book, and nudge Izzy with it. She flinches, as if it were a tarantula in my hand, but then relaxes and gives me a questioning look.

"This was in that box that was left at my mom's store. Remember?"

"Yes...," Izzy says slowly.

"Read this." I open to the inscription and set the book on her desk. As Izzy reads, I notice Cam peering over, obviously interested. I would share with her too, but then other classmates might wonder what we're talking about, and it would turn into a whole thing. I want this to be about just me and Izzy.

"Okay?" Izzy says, pushing the book away. She wipes her hand on her skirt and says, "I don't really get it. Someone wrote in an old book? Is your mom mad about it or something?"

"No, no." I shake my head. "Did you notice the names? One of them is Susie."

This doesn't clear up anything for Izzy, so I say, "Like: Grandma Susie? I'm wondering if that message was written by Jacuzzi!"

Izzy nods, finally understanding. "Well, that would make sense if she was the one who left the box."

"But she wasn't the one to leave—"

I don't finish what I'm saying, though, because Izzy turns away to talk to Link.

I'm not sure what I hoped Izzy would say or do when I showed her the inscription, but that wasn't it. Her nonreaction feels like a kicked bruise. I return the book to my backpack.

Nell walks in right before the second bell rings. Her hair is up in double buns with bright yellow flowers tucked in each, and she's wearing a crocheted sweater I'd bet she made herself. She gives me a wave from across the room, and I point to my own head where her buns would be and mouth, *Cute.* She smiles and takes off her backpack and sits at her desk, chatting with the kids near her.

Mr. Orson tells us to break into our groups for the storytelling project, and my stomach begins to ache again. We've avoided talking about *Shellfish Holmes* so far, but we can't avoid it now. Are Link and Ben and Cam doing it with us? Is it even still happening?

I act like I have to finish writing something in my notebook, stalling to see what Izzy does first. Right now, I envy Nell working by herself. She doesn't have to worry about anything. Across the room, she's flipping through drawing after drawing of women's fashion in her sketchbook until she gets to a blank page to start a new one. She's probably blissfully humming to herself and not at all anxious about what she's doing.

"Leave space for Maizy," I hear behind me, and glance back to see Ben, Link, Cam, and Izzy waiting for me to slide my desk next to theirs. *Relief.*

"So," Ben says right off the bat, "the plan is a lobster detective story, right?" He's looking at me, and there's something about this that breaks my spell of uncertainty. I might be confused about my friendship with Izzy, but I'm not confused about my lobster detective story. I understand *that* completely.

"Sure. If everyone wants to," I reply modestly. It's a group project, after all, so I want everyone to be on board.

"Of course we do," Izzy says. She holds my gaze for a second. We may not have said a word about what happened on Saturday, but I feel like there's an apology in her eyes. Or at least a *Let's move past this.*

I smile, even though I'm still not sure how I feel about everything.

"We should read through the script and decide who wants to play which parts." I hand out the two copies and say, "I'll make more, but for now we can share."

Link starts reading the script out loud. He's a bit monotone and serious—I imagined Shellfish Holmes a little more energetic—but I listen and let him do his thing. When Shellfish introduces himself to another character, Ben interrupts.

"You know what he should say?" Ben grabs the script from Link and crosses out a line of my dialogue. I frown. I know this is a group project, but it's kind of insulting to have spent a lot of time on something and have Ben make changes without at least a discussion, let alone listening to the whole script first.

Link leans over and reads out loud what Ben wrote. "*I'm Holmes, Shellfish Holmes.* Ha! Love it."

"Genius, right?" Ben says.

Genius?! I'd hardly say a knockoff of a famous line is *genius*. I mean, Shellfish Holmes is a knockoff of a famous character, but I'm not the one going around calling myself a genius.

"I don't think that really works," I try to explain. "That's more of a James Bond thing than Sherlock—"

"And we need a fight sequence," Link adds.

"Fight sequence?" I repeat.

Ben jabs a finger at Link and says, "*Yes!* Absolutely. What about this…"

He flips open his notebook and starts writing.

Mr. Orson stops by our group. He's on the young side for a teacher, with a goatee, and he likes to wear flannel shirts with bookish tees underneath. Today's has a drawing of a spaceship and reads, "Take Me to Your Reader."

"How's it going here? Did you guys settle on an idea?" he asks.

"We're doing a mix of genres," Izzy says. "Comedy and mystery."

"And action," Ben says.

"Yeah, it's about a secret agent lobster," Link says.

"Detective, not a secret agent," I clarify.

"His name is Shellfish Holmes," Ben says.

Mr. Orson laughs, which makes me feel good, until he addresses Ben and says, "Great idea!"

And Link says, "Thanks."

Just: *Thanks.*

That's it.

"Sounds like a lot of fun!" Mr. Orson says, and moves on to another group.

The boys lean back together, planning out their fight scene. I'm too stunned to do much but sit and stare at them.

"You basically took credit for Maizy's idea. You know that, right?" Cam says.

I want to slap my hands on my desk and shout, *THANK YOU!*

"Who did?" Ben asks.

"You did," Cam says, calmly outlining a maze in the margin of her paper. "Both of you."

"No, we didn't," Link says.

"When did we do that?" Ben asks. It's the first time I've seen smiley Ben not look so smiley.

"Just now, when Mr. Orson was here. He said you had a good idea, and you said thanks."

Link rolls his eyes. "He said *we* had a good idea. I was saying thanks on behalf of all of us."

"You didn't say Maizy came up with it. That's basically the same as taking credit."

"Oh, come on," Ben says. "What does it matter who came up with the idea, anyway?"

I should probably say something and stand up for myself, but I'm at a loss for words. And I'm also wondering if Ben's right. Does it matter who came up with the idea? If it doesn't matter, then why did it not feel great just a minute ago when I wasn't factored into the conversation with Mr. Orson at all?

"I didn't hear Ben or Link take credit for anything," Izzy chimes in. "Mr. Orson asked questions, and they answered. Let's just get back to work on the project."

Somehow, this feels worse than Ben and Link taking over my script and not crediting me for the idea. Izzy is acting like nothing happened all over again. Izzy, my best friend. I can't take it anymore.

I stand up.

"What are you doing?" Izzy asks.

"I'm doing something else."

"C'mon, Maizy," Ben says. "Be a team player. This is a group project."

I must give Ben a look that feels like lasers, because he flinches. *I'm* the one not being a team player? I wrote an entire script, and we didn't even make it through half a page before they took my idea and ran with it in another direction. They didn't even ask about my plot or discuss as a group if *we* wanted a fight scene. How is *that* being a team player? Am I supposed to let them walk all over me and not complain?

"What are you going to do? Work by yourself?" Link asks.

"I don't know. Maybe."

Izzy sighs, like she's dealing with a stubborn child. "Maizy, you can do your own thing if you want, but this group is doing *Shellfish Holmes*. You can't abandon us *and* force us to start from scratch too."

I stare at Izzy. I just don't know who she is anymore.

"You can have the Shellfish Holmes idea, but you can't have my script." I grab the pages. "Not that you were using it anyway."

I drag my desk away from theirs.

"Maizy," Izzy says.

And I actually hope, despite everything, that she's going to say *Don't go*, or that she's sorry, or that we should go back to our original group of two. But when I look back at her, I don't see Izzy anymore. I see Isabelle, and she's not happy with me. Again.

I can visualize this moment the way I'd shoot it in one of my movies: The rest of the class, buzzing and bustling around us, freezes mid-action. The lights dim, throwing everyone in shadow except me and Izzy.

"Good luck on your own," she says.

She means more than the class project.

I blink, then blink again.

"You too," I reply.

8

Time to Regroup

I NEED TO TELL MR. ORSON I'M SWITCHING PROJECTS, BUT NELL IS AT his desk showing her sketchbook when I walk up, so I stand back and wait. I'm numb from what just happened, and watching Nell flip through fashion sketch after fashion sketch is oddly soothing.

"Ten outfits?" Mr. Orson says. "That's a lot."

"Oh, I don't mind," Nell says. "I love to sew. Half of these are already put together, anyway."

"Well, I'm glad you're up to the challenge, but I also mean it sounds like a lot to squeeze into the ten-minute limit. Maybe you could trim it down?"

"But the idea is women's fashion through the twentieth *century*. I need at least one look for each decade."

"Why not focus on one decade instead? Pick your favorite."

Nell considers this. "And I could do an outfit from each year…"

"No, that would bring you back to ten outfits." Mr. Orson indicates me waiting and says, "While I help Maizy, why don't you brainstorm ways you can simplify your idea."

Nell takes her sketchbook back to her desk, and Mr. Orson turns to me.

I don't want to explain what happened with my group. I just want to move on, so I cut right to the chase.

"I've decided to do a different topic for the project."

"Something different?" Mr. Orson says. "You only have two weeks left. Are you sure you want to start something new?"

No, I'm not sure, I think to myself. But I don't feel like I have a choice.

"I already have an idea," I say.

Mr. Orson nods encouragingly. "All right, let's hear it!"

Shoot. I was hoping he wouldn't ask that.

"Umm…" My mind casts about wildly for other story ideas—I've had a million of them, but of course I can't remember a single one now. I blurt out the only other thing that's been on my mind this weekend.

"Nancy Drew."

"Nancy Drew?" Mr. Orson repeats. "Could you elaborate?"

I gulp and start babbling, the idea unfolding as I talk.

"Well, my mom owns Alter Ego, that thrift store downtown. And someone left a box of Nancy Drew books there last weekend, and inside was a photo of my grandmother. We thought she left them, but she says she didn't, so it's a big mystery who did, and I was thinking I could do some kind of documentary-style project about Nancy Drew and these books appearing and trying to get to the bottom of why they showed up…"

Mr. Orson is squinting, like he's trying hard to follow me. I have no idea if I'm making any sense. Then he asks, "Would you and Cam be making the documentary together?"

"Me and Cam?" I'm about to say *Why Cam?* when I realize she's standing behind me. I'm not sure how long she's been there. "Oh. Hey, Cam."

I brace myself for everything to fall apart now. Cam is probably going to tell Mr. Orson what happened, and he'll probably make us work together as a group and find a compromise...

But Cam says, "I'd love to do a documentary about Nancy Drew. That sounds way better than what they're doing. They decided to rename their movie *Smellfish Holmes*."

"*Smell*fish?!" I repeat. My mouth hangs open in disbelief.

"Yup." Cam nods. "They think it's hysterical. A detective who smells horribly fishy."

Mr. Orson chortles, then quickly clears his throat and resumes his neutral teacher face. Across the room, the boys are acting out a scene for Izzy.

Link leans close to Ben, a suspicious *What were you doing on the night of the murder?* look on his face. Ben grasps his nose and flings himself to the floor in response, and they both burst out in laughter. Izzy smiles and laughs too, but it's her polite laugh, not her genuine, caught-off-guard laugh.

My mouth is still hanging open when Nell rushes up.

"Mr. Orson, I know what I can do!"

"Great," he says. "Let's hear it."

"I'll have a changing area on the stage. I'm thinking something on wheels so it's easy to roll out, with curtains on all sides. And there will be music to go with each decade, and the lights can change too—you know, to adjust the mood for each look—"

"Weren't you brainstorming how to simplify your plan?" Mr. Orson says.

"Yes! I was about to get to that part. I'll record voice-overs of myself talking about the fashion in each decade. And then while I'm changing, the voice-over plays and voilà! I step out and show the look, then step back in."

"But…" Mr. Orson tugs at his goatee.

"The voice-overs will make it simpler, see? And it won't take as much time if I don't have to go on and off the stage to change."

"I admire your ambition, Nell, but I think you might need to save this idea for Broadway."

"But…" Nell blinks rapidly. "What am I supposed to do if I don't do this?"

Mr. Orson looks from Nell to me to Cam. "Why don't you three work together? Maybe there's a way to incorporate fashion into the Nancy Drew documentary? How does that sound?"

"Umm…" I see the slightest flash of hurt on Nell's face when I hesitate to agree. It's not because of Nell or Cam. It's that I'm still feeling a little shocked at myself walking away from Izzy and the Shellfish Holmes project. But I have no real plan, and I appreciate that Cam spoke up for me, and Nell is super nice…"Yeah, that would be great!"

In case Nell needs some convincing, I add, "Nancy Drew is very fashionable. We could include something about what she wears in different books."

Nell's face brightens. "That's true! Okay, that could be fun…"

Mr. Orson claps his hands, satisfied by this outcome. "Okay! Looks like you've all got yourself a new group."

A new group. I glance across the room at Izzy. Isabelle. Her arms are crossed while Ben and Link talk animatedly with each other, and I can't tell if she's bored or annoyed. She shifts in her seat and sees me watching, then immediately leans forward, acting like she's laughing about something they just said. It's obvious she's faking it. And oddly enough, as angry as I am with her, as ridiculous as I think she's being, I can't help feeling a little sad that this is how things are right now.

But I can't do anything about that, so I focus instead on Nell and Cam, and together we start making plans for a Nancy Drew documentary. I'm not sure what Cam heard me tell Mr. Orson, so I fill her in on the box of books, the photo, and the inscription.

"The strange thing is, my grandmother says she knows nothing about the books and didn't recognize the photo."

Nell taps her pen to her lips thoughtfully. "Maybe that's true, and it's a coincidence?"

"I guess...," I say.

"Or...maybe the books were left by her evil twin!" Cam says. "And it's a secret message. Or a threat!"

"Um..." I'm pretty sure Cam is joking, but it's hard to tell with her. "I don't think my grandmother has a twin. But maybe?"

Cam snaps her fingers. "I have a great idea," she says. "My mom watches this true-crime show that Link and I aren't supposed to watch, but I sometimes do, and the screen will say 'This is a reenactment.' In the documentary, we can re-create the moment when the box was left and you found it."

We all like this idea, so Nell writes it down.

"We should also learn more about Nancy Drew," I say.

"And what she wore," Nell adds. "We can do an image search for covers."

"We should go to the library to do research," Cam suggests.

As we brainstorm together, I remember Kelsey, that college girl at Turn the Page. She suggested that

I talk to her professor about the old Nancy Drew books, and the slip of paper with Kelsey's email is still tucked in one of the books at home. Originally, the idea of meeting with a college professor intimidated me, but if it's the three of us and for our documentary…

I mention the possibility of this interview, and Cam and Nell like the idea, so I make a note to email Kelsey when I get home. We also decide Nell will take the lead on researching Nancy Drew fashion, Cam is in charge of researching her history, and I will start a script, narrating the story of what led us to this project, as well as create a list of shots we might want to include in the documentary. The three of us make a plan to go to the Larksville Library later in the week, and we continue sharing ideas until the bell rings.

9

Change on the Horizon

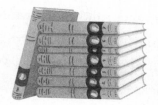

AFTER SCHOOL, I GET TO WORK ON A NEW SCRIPT, SINCE WE ONLY HAVE two weeks remaining to plan, write, research, interview, film, and edit. I also email Kelsey. She replies almost immediately with "Super! So happy you reached out. I'll check with Professor Vale and get back to you soon with options for when she can meet."

The next day, there's nobody waiting for me at the bench. You'd think Izzy—Isabelle—and I had never met, by the way we interact. Or don't interact, I guess.

Nell and I both brought in books from our Nancy Drew collections to share and look through. We decided all three of us should read at least a few Nancy Drew books to get familiar with them. Cam picks *The Secret at Shadow Ranch* from my stack and starts reading, while Nell gets busy making notes about Nancy's different fashion looks from her illustrated covers. I spend part of class drafting ideas for the script and part of the class reading more of *The Message in the Hollow Oak*.

"Is that the one with the inscription?" Nell asks, and when I nod she says, "Have you shown it to Jacuzzi yet?"

"Not yet, but she's coming over for dinner, so I'll show her tonight."

"Can I see it?" Cam asks, and I flip to the page with the message from Susie.

She brushes a finger over the ink. "1959! Do you think she'll remember it?"

"I don't know, but I bet she'll be just as curious as I am about why it showed up," I reply.

We continue to work together comfortably but without much chatter. I try my best to ignore

Isabelle's laugh whenever I hear it from across the room.

At lunch I discover an origami club meeting, which seems like a good alternative to eating by myself. It ends up being thirty minutes of silent paper folding.

Life is feeling pretty quiet without Izzy.

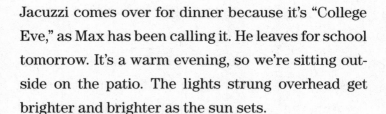

Jacuzzi comes over for dinner because it's "College Eve," as Max has been calling it. He leaves for school tomorrow. It's a warm evening, so we're sitting outside on the patio. The lights strung overhead get brighter and brighter as the sun sets.

I'm restlessly reading *The Message in the Hollow Oak*, waiting for a good time to show Jacuzzi the inscription. At the moment, she's looking at photos on Max's phone of what his dorm will be like. Mom's inside mixing up a salad. Dad is by the grill, testing out his apron-shelf invention, which is exactly what it sounds like: an apron with a shelf that protrudes at belly-button level. He calls it the Belf, which I told him is a horrible name.

It sounds too much like *belch*. But he's sticking with it unless he thinks of something better. A bowl of sauce and a pair of tongs sit on the Belf. It has a tacky top to help them stay in place, but he doesn't trust it enough yet to lean forward. Instead, he moves up and down, like a barbecue-swabbing elevator.

When Jacuzzi hands Max back his phone, I seize the moment.

"Jacuzzi, I have to show you something." I flip to the inscription and hand the book over. I'm anticipating that her reaction will be something like pressing her hand to her heart and cooing, "I remember Annette!" And maybe she'll tell me stories about the Nancy Drew Detective Agency she and her best friend started when they were ten.

But in reality, Jacuzzi reads the inscription silently. She nods ever so slightly, hands the book back, and says, "That's an interesting find!"

Then she turns to Max and begins to ask him something.

I interrupt. "But, Jacuzzi…"

I don't want to be rude, but she must not have looked at the inscription carefully.

"Did you recognize that book? Do you see the name signed inside?"

When she doesn't say anything, I continue. "*Susie!* Someone named Susie gave that book to her friend in 1959. I thought it could have been you."

Jacuzzi looks like she's debating saying something as Mom opens the sliding glass door and steps outside with the salad.

"We're almost ready here," Dad says from the grill. He squats, slowly and stiffly, to brush more barbecue sauce on the chicken.

Jacuzzi scoots her chair closer, making room for Mom, and finally replies to me. "Susie was a popular name when I was young," she says. "There was probably another Susie who gave that book to a friend."

"Did you have a friend named Annette?" I ask.

"I'm not really sure," Jacuzzi murmurs. When I look at her in disbelief, she adds, "That was a long time ago."

I guess, but...Could you forget someone you once thanked for a million little things? Will I forget Izzy sixty years from now? Even if we stop being friends and never talk again? It's hard to believe I could forget her.

I thought for sure I was onto something. And I'm still not convinced I'm wrong—the thing is, even if the young Susie who wrote in this book was not my grandmother, it's the sort of coincidence my Jacuzzi would ordinarily revel in. My Jacuzzi is someone who delights in the unexpected and finds wonder in small moments. She would have gasped and exclaimed *What are the chances?* and spun stories with me about who (or what!) could have brought those books to Alter Ego. The fact that Jacuzzi instead seems so...uninterested...makes me feel something is off with her.

A fly circles my head, and I swat it away. Dad dishes up the chicken, we pass around the salad bowl, and then we all raise our glasses to toast Max and his new adventure.

"Are you nervous to be on your own?" Jacuzzi asks my brother.

He shrugs. "Not really." Then he jokes, "Maybe about the dorm food, though."

Jacuzzi laughs and says, "What about you, Maizy?"

"Me?"

Does she want to know if I'd be nervous about dorm food too?

"What about me?"

"Are you ready?" Jacuzzi asks.

I must still look confused because Jacuzzi explains. "With Max gone, it will be a new adventure for you too."

The sky rumbles softly, prompting me to look up at the far-off dark clouds creeping closer. There's been so much talk and planning about Max leaving for college, I haven't really thought about the after part.

"I guess I'm ready?"

"You'll have your mom and me all to yourself," Dad says.

"No more fighting over the bathroom in the morning," Mom adds.

"You'll finally get your only-child experience," Max adds.

"Finally," I say, and laugh with everyone else, even though it doesn't feel funny.

Thunder rumbles again.

"It's not supposed to rain, is it?" Mom asks.

"I don't think so," Jacuzzi replies.

But I feel a drop on my arm before she finishes her sentence. Then another.

"Uh-oh." Dad shifts his chair back, and we all start grabbing dishes and napkins and silverware and the salad bowl as the drops pelt all around us, faster and faster as we hurry to the sliding door. Jacuzzi can't run with her walking boot, so Max unzips his hoodie and holds it over her head until they reach the door.

Once inside, we turn with our arms still full and stare at raindrops hopping around like they're celebrating having the patio to themselves. The Belf was left behind on the ground.

"Poor Belf," Max says.

"Well, good thing it's waterproof," Dad replies.

Everyone else turns toward the kitchen, but I stay at the window, frowning at the raindrops. It had been a perfectly clear, warm evening. Nobody saw that coming.

In the kitchen, Jacuzzi says, "I hate to cut this party short, but I think I need an early bedtime tonight."

She asks Dad to drive her home, and he says, "No problem. Max and I have a big day tomorrow too, so extra rest would be a good idea for everyone."

"Are you feeling okay, Mom?" my mom asks Jacuzzi.

"Of course, of course." Jacuzzi gives us all hugs and an extra one for Max, wishing him good luck at college.

After Dad and Jacuzzi leave, Mom goes upstairs to take a bath. Max's friends are coming to pick him up later for a College Eve outing, but right now it's just the two of us in the kitchen. I sit on a stool at the island, twisting the seat from side to side. Max drums his fingers on the counter. Water is running upstairs for Mom's bath, and the refrigerator hums on and then off. I could go do something else, but I don't want to. Jacuzzi's question—*Are you ready?*—comes back to me. This time I hear my response loud and clear: *No, I'm not.*

"You know what we need?" Max finally says. "Bologna-cheese melts."

"Seriously? We just ate dinner."

"I'm always serious about bologna-cheese melts."

I'm not hungry, and my brother's infamous sandwich isn't my favorite, but it occurs to me I might not see another bologna-cheese melt in our house until Thanksgiving.

"All right," I say.

After microwaving the sandwiches for twelve seconds—he swears by that as the optimal time to get the cheese melty but not hard—he presses the whole thing down with his palm. I've told him before that it's gross to put your hand all over something if you're giving it to another person to eat. In response, Max licked the entire side of my sandwich before passing it to me.

I don't say anything tonight.

We eat our sandwiches in silence. When Max is finished, he crumples his paper towel and asks, "Want to play Fruit Frenzy?"

Lately it has been me asking Max to play the game, not the other way around.

"Sure," I say.

Maybe I'm not the only one feeling nostalgic for things that are about to change.

10

The Missing Author

EARLY THE NEXT MORNING, WE GATHER OUTSIDE BEFORE DAD AND MAX get in the car. It's a two-hour drive to Max's college. Dad will help him get settled and take him out to dinner, stay overnight, and drive back tomorrow.

Mom hands my brother a shopping bag. "Cleaning supplies," she says. "For your dorm room. Make sure you clean everything first, even if it already looks clean."

And then she gets teary and hugs him tight, squishing the bag between them. Max looks at me over Mom's head and rolls his eyes, but not in a genuinely annoyed way.

When it's our turn to say goodbye, Max says, "Any time you want to play Fruit Frenzy, let me know."

I nod. "I will. Don't eat too many bologna and cheese."

"It's impossible to eat too many bologna and cheese."

He gives me a proper hug, and that's it. Dad hugs me and Mom, and then they're in the car, on their way.

I know things won't be the same without Max around, but it doesn't seem that way yet. This morning doesn't feel much different from when his high school classes started earlier than mine, so he left first.

Sometimes big changes happen in small moments, I guess.

Later that day, Nell shows up to Mr. Orson's class wearing a bell-shaped felt hat with a flower on the side. She tells me and Cam it's called a cloche.

"Nancy wore something like this on one of the covers of *The Secret of the Old Clock*. It's a style that was popular in the 1920s. I could make us each one, if you want."

"I don't wear hats," Cam says.

"Never?" Nell asks.

"Maybe a knit cap if it's snowing, but that's it."

I can tell Nell is disappointed Cam isn't more excited to wear a cloche, so I say, "Maybe just for the project you could wear a hat?" But the deadpan face Cam gives me says that's not going to happen.

"Well, I'll wear one, anyway," I say to Nell.

"Great!" she says. "I also noticed a lot of silky scarves on different Nancy Drew covers, Cam. I'll find you a scarf instead."

In response, Cam dramatically face-plants onto her folded arms, making Nell and me giggle.

I make it through another Izzy-less day and another silent lunch with the origami club—I'm getting pretty good at folding frogs.

And things keep moving along with the Nancy Drew project. After school, there's a message from Kelsey letting me know we can interview her professor this Saturday, so I coordinate a time with Cam and Nell. And Thursday after school, we meet at the bike racks and ride to the Larksville Library to do more Nancy Drew research.

When we pass Jacuzzi's house, I wave, even though she's not outside. We lock our bikes under a tree. Cam picks up an acorn that's perfectly whole and still a bit green. When I was little and sometimes spent a day with Jacuzzi, we walked up and down this street and collected acorns by the bucketful. Cam tosses hers and catches it as we walk through the sliding glass doors. The cold blast of air-conditioning instantly chills the sweat on my face.

We huddle under a banner advertising the library's upcoming used-book fair at Larksville Park and debate where to go to learn more about Nancy Drew. Mystery, children's, history, reference? We decide on the children's section because it's the closest. We pass a train table that's not being played with. Cam sets her acorn inside a tunnel.

"A treasure for someone to find," she explains. That's something Jacuzzi would do too.

The author of the books is Carolyn Keene, so we search the "K" aisle until we find *Keene.* I was expecting a collection of the older Nancy Drew books, like the ones I found in the box, but there aren't any like that. Instead, there's a variety of paperbacks that look more recent, although they don't look like they go together.

Cam pulls out three different ones and reads from the covers. "'Nancy Drew Diaries,' 'Nancy Drew: Girl Detective,' 'The Nancy Drew Notebooks'…There are so many different series about her!"

Nell pulls another off the shelf. "The Nancy Drew Clue Book series! I read those in second grade. I completely forgot about them." She flips through the pages, a light smile on her face.

"It's kind of hard to believe your grandmother read about this character when she was ten, and here we are, how many years later, and kids today are still reading about her," Cam says.

"That's it!" I snap my fingers and point to Cam. "You're brilliant!"

Cam shrugs. "Thanks."

"Wait, why?" Nell says. "No offense—I'm not saying you're not brilliant, Cam. I'm just missing something."

"I am too," Cam says. "No offense taken."

"What you said about how my grandmother read Nancy Drew as a kid and kids today are still reading about her," I explain. "Why has Nancy Drew stuck around for so long? That can be the question our documentary explores."

Cam nods. "I like that: How did Carolyn Keene create a character who has stayed popular for decades?"

"Yeah," Nell agrees. She holds up the book she was flipping through. "This is number fifteen in the Clue Book series, and there are books from at least four different series on this shelf. Not to mention all the older books that aren't even here—Carolyn Keene has probably written a hundred books already!"

"Way more than that," a voice pipes up behind us. "More like a thousand."

Spinning around, the three of us say in unison, "A *thousand*?!"

A teenage boy with a full book cart is standing there.

"Do you work here?" Cam asks, arms crossed and sounding a little suspicious.

"I volunteer," he replies.

"Hmmm." Cam doesn't seem convinced.

"I'm Calvin." The boy slides a book into its spot on the shelf. "And you are?"

"We're Maizy, Nell, and Cam," I reply, pointing to each of us in turn.

"Like Nancy, Bess, and George, the characters in the books?" Calvin asks.

"Ummm…" The three of us look at one another. I have to admit, I kind of like the association. Nell nods, and Cam shrugs, which I think is their way of indicating they kind of like it too. "I guess?"

"Are you solving a mystery?"

"Yeah, the mystery of how this lady wrote a thousand books," Cam replies. "That can't be right."

"Correct," Calvin says, backing his cart out of the aisle to put away the rest of his books elsewhere.

"But didn't you just say she wrote that many?" Nell calls after him. "And now you're saying she didn't?"

"He's messing with us," Cam says.

Calvin's gone without an answer.

"Hello?" I call. "Did she or didn't she write that many books?"

I follow after him.

"You're asking the wrong question," Calvin says over his shoulder as he continues walking away. "You should be asking: *Does Carolyn Keene exist?*"

He turns down another aisle and disappears.

"Forget him," Cam says. "He's just wasting our time. Let's go find a real librarian. She'll help us find the info we need."

Calvin's head pops out of the aisle, and Nell yelps.

"*He.* The reference librarian is who you are looking for, and they are a *he.* My uncle Marty, actually. And you should know he hates Nancy Drew. With a passion."

And then he disappears again.

"What's he trying to be, a book magician?" Cam mumbles.

She and Nell are both ready to go find the

reference librarian, but I'm stuck on the question Calvin posed.

"Does Carolyn Keene exist?" I ask into the empty space where he just stood. There's no reply, so I jog around the corner and find him at the end of the row, crouched low, shelving a book.

"So does she exist?" I ask again, coming to a halt next to him.

Calvin stands. He's quite a bit taller than I am, nearly as tall as Max. He leans forward, like he's about to confide something top secret, and whispers, "No."

I throw my hands in the air, exasperated. "Who wrote the books, then? Her ghost?"

Finally, he stops toying with us and explains. "Carolyn Keene is a pseudonym. That's why she doesn't exist. Or she exists, but only as an idea. In reality, she's a bunch of different people who have written the Nancy Drew books over the years."

I'm not sure why this disappoints me, but it does. Maybe because I've read enough Nancy Drews now that I've formed an idea of what Carolyn Keene would be like. I was imagining her as a sharp-witted woman about Jacuzzi's age who went for a run every morning before sitting down to write the next chapter in her latest Nancy Drew mystery. She'd break for lunch and walk her dog and then write another chapter in the afternoon. And she always had a small notepad and pencil with her no matter where she went, because she never knew when inspiration might strike.

"Well, it does make more sense if she's not real," Nell says. "I was starting to wonder how old she must be."

I hadn't thought about the math, but now that Nell points this out, I realize that if some of the books I found in the box were published in 1930, then Carolyn Keene would have to be over one hundred if she was still writing books today.

"So why does your uncle the librarian hate Nancy Drew?" Cam asks.

"Yeah, I didn't think librarians were allowed to hate books," I add.

Calvin gives me a look like I've said the most ridiculous thing ever. "No book is for everybody."

Which reminds me that my mom isn't a fan of Nancy Drew books either, although she hasn't actually read any. "Has your uncle even read them?"

Calvin shrugs. "Ask him."

The three of us leave Calvin and head to the reference desk to find out more. Based on Calvin's description of Uncle Marty the Librarian as someone who passionately hates Nancy Drew, I imagined he'd be old and cranky. The type who would shush someone for sneezing. But he's younger than I guessed—more like my parents' age. And he smiles pleasantly when we approach his desk. He adjusts his round-frame glasses, brushes something invisible off his button-down shirt, and straightens his cardigan.

"Can I help you?"

"Yes, um, we need to research…" I take a breath, a little bit worried that saying this name will unleash a different side to the pleasant-seeming Uncle Marty the Librarian. "Nancy Drew," I say in a rush.

There's no outburst or outrage. All Uncle Marty the Librarian does is say, "Certainly!" He types into his computer. "Is there a particular aspect of Nancy Drew you're interested in researching?"

"Fashion," Nell replies. When he looks at her questioningly, she explains. "How her style has changed over the years."

"Ah." He nods.

"We're also interested in the history behind the books," Cam adds. "How the series got started and that kind of stuff."

He nods and keeps typing. "I think we have just the thing."

Uncle Marty—or Martin Noys, as the name badge on his lanyard reads—leads us through the library. He has very good posture. The kind that makes me pull back my shoulders and straighten up as we follow him. We pass Calvin shelving more books, and Uncle Marty gives him the barest of nods.

"I think that nephew of yours was messing with us, Mr. Noys," Cam says as we walk. "Is he even your nephew?"

"Calvin? Oh yes, he is. How was he messing with you?"

"He said you hate Nancy Drew," Nell answers.

Cam adds, "With a passion."

Still bright and chirpy, Mr. Noys replies, "Oh yes,

I do. That's true." He drags a finger along a row of book spines until he finds the one he's looking for. "Here you go! This should tell you everything you want to know about Nancy Drew."

Nell accepts the book, and Cam looks from it to him. "So...why don't you like her? Nancy Drew?"

"Oh, it's not personal. I don't dislike Nancy Drew per se, but my recollection of the books is that the mysteries are...what's the word I'm looking for?" He pauses, like we might know and be able to tell him, then snaps his fingers. "Ridiculous. They're ridiculous. Nancy's intuition never steers her wrong, and one convenient thing after another happens."

I disagree that the books are ridiculous, but he's also not wrong. The titles I've read *do* rely on Nancy's intuition and a lot of coincidences to solve the mysteries, but they're a lot of fun too. It's almost comedic to me, those elements of the story, and I'm always curious how things will turn out.

"Nancy Drew is skilled at everything she tries to do," he adds. "It's a little too good to be true."

A teenage girl who's capable of anything she puts her mind to is "too good to be true"? I wonder if Mr.

Noys would say the same about Sherlock Holmes or James Bond.

"What's the problem with that?" I ask.

"Nothing. Nothing." He steps back slightly. "To each his own."

"Or her own," Nell adds.

"Of course!" Mr. Noys takes off his glasses and uses a corner of his cardigan to clean them. "Well then, I'll be at my desk if you need more help finding books."

He hurries off. Before the three of us say anything to one another, Calvin pipes up behind us again. "Told you he's a grump about Nancy Drew."

And Nell yelps a second time.

"Were you lurking in the bookshelves?" Cam asks.

"I'm always lurking in the bookshelves. I volunteer here. That's what I'm not paid to do."

Cam checks out *On the Case of Nancy Drew*, the book Mr. Noys found for us. When we step outside the library, I notice Jacuzzi's garage door going up. "Jacuzzi!" I call, but I don't think she hears.

"Who are you waving to?" Cam asks.

"My grandmother." I point to the small yellow house on the other side of the street. "That's where she lives."

Jacuzzi is dressed in a flowy black dress, with one flat shoe and her tall black walking boot. I'm used to her playful way of dressing, so it's odd to see her wearing something so simple and all in one color.

"I hope she's not driving somewhere," I say. "She's not supposed to do that."

"Why can't she drive?" Nell asks.

"She broke her foot," I explain. "Or fractured it, I guess. Her doctor says the walking boot might make it difficult to drive a car safely."

I shift uneasily, wondering if I should text my mom. But that feels like tattling, so I don't.

"It doesn't seem like she's getting in her car," Nell says.

"You're right. She must have needed something from the garage." I'm glad I didn't text Mom and get her worked up over nothing.

We turn away, heading to our bikes, but something is still seeming not quite right about Jacuzzi. I'm not sure why. Maybe because I've never seen her dressed like that? Maybe because I'm still worried about the possibility of her driving?

I look back, and Jacuzzi isn't in her car. Instead, she's coasting down her driveway on a bike, her frilly black dress ruffling in the wind and a purple helmet on her head.

⑪

A Chase in the Park

"JACUZZI HAS A BIKE?" I'VE NEVER SEEN HER ON ONE IN MY LIFE. "SHE knows how to ride it?"

Nell and Cam are watching too.

"That is a horrible outfit for a bike ride," Cam adds.

I'm about to say, *Better than a lobster suit,* but panic zips through me. *Is* it better? I can imagine the dress getting caught in the spokes, just like my lobster tail. Does Jacuzzi know that could happen? If she falls, she won't have all the plush padding I

had for protection. Wait—forget the plush padding—
if she falls, she could reinjure her foot!

Jacuzzi shrinks into a smaller and smaller speck
down the street. I hurry to unlock my bike.

"I need to follow her and make sure everything
is okay," I say.

"Hang on, we'll go with you," Nell says, unloop-
ing her lock.

Cam clicks on her helmet, and the three of us
pedal off.

Jacuzzi rides with purpose. If she wasn't wearing a flowy dress, I would think she'd thrown herself
into a new exercise routine. Her foot clearly isn't
bothered by the pedaling, at least. She turns left at
the end of the block.

"I don't want to lose sight of her," I call to Cam
and Nell, and we pump our legs harder in an effort
to catch up.

I spot her once we make the turn, but she's way
far ahead. She's already crossing Main Street, and
there are at least ten houses between us. We get
stuck at the light and have to wait to cross. I push
my palm repeatedly against the button.

"Should we call for her to stop?" Nell asks.

I hesitate, and I'm not sure why. I'm worried about Jacuzzi, but also, she's been acting odd. Ever since that box of Nancy Drew books showed up, she's seemed not quite herself. At least in how she reacted to the photo and the inscription I found. And now a midday bike ride in fancy attire? Nancy Drew would definitely find this suspicious, and so do I.

"Let's just keep an eye on her for now," I say.

"Easier said than done," Cam says as Jacuzzi bears left behind the shops onto the path that leads into Larksville Park.

"Oh, come on!" I press the button rapidly, even though I know it doesn't make a difference. Or maybe it does, because the crossing signal changes and beeps for us. We pedal fast. The park is huge— it stretches for blocks behind the restaurants and stores on Main Street. It's hilly and filled with lots of paths. Once Jacuzzi takes a couple of turns, we'll be lucky to find her again.

We round behind the shops, riding along the giant field used for sports during the day and outdoor concerts at night. There's a community center on the opposite side of the field, with a pool and an outdoor skating rink for the winter.

Jacuzzi isn't on the path to the community center, and I think we've already lost her until Nell points.

"There she is! By the fountain!"

Jacuzzi coasts around the fountain, then pedals past one of the playgrounds. We see her turn onto the path that winds through the demonstration garden. It leads to the small lake on the far side of the park. Beyond the lake is a border of tall evergreens that separates the park from the wealthy neighborhoods of Larksville.

"Maybe she's going to the Lark?" Cam suggests.

The Lark! That's the fancy restaurant on the lake. The dress would make more sense if that's where Jacuzzi is going. And sure enough, once the Lark is in our view, we see Jacuzzi at the bike rack across the path, removing her helmet and fixing her hair. She crosses the path and heads inside.

"It's kind of early for dinner," Cam observes.

That's true. I want to go inside and see what she's doing.

We lock our bikes next to Jacuzzi's and cross the path to the restaurant, devising a plan to go in and ask to use the bathroom. They might tell us to use the public one down by the dock where the paddleboat rentals are, but we figure it'll at least buy us time to scope out the place. And if Jacuzzi is right inside and sees us, then we can act like it's a huge coincidence running into her.

It takes a minute for my eyes to adjust when we step through the front door. I've never been inside the Lark, and there's a huge window straight ahead with a view of the lake. The sun glints off the water, adding to the blinding effect. The restaurant is even fancier than I imagined, with the distant tinkle of calming piano music and lots of grownups in dressy black attire mingling in the bar area with wineglasses.

Nell, Cam, and I stay close together and move forward like a school of fish. The three of us are so out of place, I half expect to hear that record-scratch sound, and the piano to cut off, and every head to turn our way. But the people are absorbed in their conversations. I can't make out Jacuzzi in this sea of black clothes and gray hair. One man separates from a group and hands me a folded piece of paper.

"Your program," he says in a soft voice.

I accept it automatically, not sure if this is a customary thing at fancy restaurants.

Nell speaks up. "We actually need to use the—"

"Finally!"

A woman strides over, three children in tow. "I called the babysitting service to see what the holdup was. Did you get lost?"

The children peer at us from behind her. The oldest is a girl who looks maybe five, and she holds the hands of boy-and-girl twins who are probably two or three.

The woman is quite tall, her height emphasized by her boxy black hat. She bends forward and exclaims, "Why did they send three of you? We only need one!"

Nell, Cam, and I look back and forth between one another, like we're checking to see if we're all on the same totally confused page. We are.

"I think you're making a—" Cam begins, but the woman pushes us gently toward the door.

"It doesn't matter now," she says. "Just entertain them on the playground, please."

The woman turns back to the children and bends even lower so she's looking the oldest in the eyes. "Go play with the sitters, now, Gabriella, and be a good girl. Help them with your brother and sister, you hear? Auntie Ruth is going back to Grandma and your mom now."

With the *clip, clip, clip* of heels across a tiled floor, the woman disappears behind the gathered group of people.

Nell, Cam, and I stare at Gabriella and her siblings. Gabriella stares right back at us. Her little sister sucks on her thumb, but the brother raises a finger and points at Cam's head. "You have purple hair!" he shouts, only it sounds like *poopa hey-yah!*

"Oh, wow." Cam takes a step back.

I scan the restaurant, my eyes fully adjusted now, but there's no sign of Jacuzzi. It's also become totally clear that the restaurant is having some sort of special event today. I look at the program that was handed to me when we came in. There's a photo of an elderly man with the words *In Loving Memory of George Winthrop* written on the front.

"Yikes," I whisper.

"What is it?" Nell asks.

I hold up the program so she and Cam can see. "I think we crashed a funeral."

Their eyes bug out.

"What do we do now?!" Nell asks.

It's the little girl who replies. "I know what to do," she says, and lunges forward to smack me on the thigh.

"Tag! You're it!"

Gabriella pushes open the restaurant door and races outside, her siblings squealing and following after.

Nell, Cam, and I remain frozen for a second, then jump into action, following the kids outside. They've all crossed the path to the otherwise-empty playground. Gabriella is running around yelling, "Tag us! Tag us, tag us!" The little boy is squatting under the slide with his hands over his eyes. And his twin sister is doing a sumo wrestler march in a slow circle, her head tilting side to side as she chants, "Party, party..."

"These kids are wild," Cam whispers.

"What should we do?" I ask.

"I guess...this!" Nell lunges at Gabriella as she approaches, and the little girl squeals and changes direction. Cam joins in, and they chase the younger girls all around the playground, while the boy—Michael, we've heard his sisters call him—continues to squat under the slide with his eyes covered.

"Can anyone find me?" he shouts every so often.

I'm still holding the *In Loving Memory* program and walk it to the trash, but I stop myself before I drop it in. I see George Winthrop's smiling face, and even though he's a stranger, it feels wrong to throw him away. Especially during his memorial service. I'll take him home to throw away there. Better yet—I'll recycle. That feels more thoughtful.

I fold up the paper and tuck it in my pocket, then turn to the playground and shout, "The ground is lava in five...four..."

Squeals erupt again, and even the little boy leaves his spot under the slide to climb up the play

structure. We all make it to safety before I get to "one," and then Cam says, "Everything but the slides is lava…," and we scramble again to huddle on a slide.

We play a few more rounds, and then Gabriella asks, "Do you want to watch me jump from up there at the top of the twisty pole?"

"No," Cam, Nell, and I say in unison.

"Jinx!" the little sister bellows. "You are a coat!"

The three of us laugh, but Gabriella throws her hands in the air. "It's *Coke*, Chloe. *You owe me a Coke!*"

But Chloe is galloping around and shouting, "Coat! Coat! Coat! You are a coat!"

I'm having fun and have forgotten what even brought us here in the first place until I see a panicked-looking teenager running from the restaurant parking lot. Her face is flushed, and she comes to a halt at the edge of the playground. "Are you the Winthrops? I'm *so* sorry I'm late!" She scans our group and says, "Wait, am I babysitting all of you? I thought there were only three."

Cam, Nell, and I all look at one another. "Gotta go!" I say to the kids, and we run to our bikes.

"Bye!" Gabriella waves after us. "Thanks for playing!"

"Come back soon!" the little boy calls.

"You are a coat!" Chloe hollers.

12

Lucky Sharm

THAT NIGHT, DAD IS BACK AND IT'S OUR FIRST DINNER WITHOUT MAX. It's probably more accurate to say it's our first dinner without Max in person, because we do a video call with him. His face is on the tablet in front of the chair where he normally sits.

"This is so weird, watching you eat," Max says.

"We won't do this every night," Mom says. "I just miss your face."

"I miss you too," Max says.

He takes us on a tour of his dorm room, which is pretty small. There's a bunk bed for him and his roommate, two desks, and two armoires. Outside is a living area and mini kitchen, a bathroom, and two more doors leading to his suitemates' rooms.

"Show them the Sharm!" Dad says.

"I should really get going," Max says. "My roommates are waiting for me to go to the dining hall."

"It will only take a second," Dad begs.

Max flicks his hair out of his face and smiles. "All right, hold on."

Our view wobbles around as Max adjusts his phone. Soon we see him in front of a bunch of clothes hung vertically on the wall. "The Sharm" stands for "shirt arm," and it's basically a hanging rod for clothes that gets attached to a wall. When it's up, all the shirts are layered on top of one another, but if Max pulls down the bar, the shirts hang the way they would in a closet. It's supposed to be useful for small spaces.

"Very nice!" Mom says.

"Nice?" Dad asks. "Or very *sharming*?" We all groan, and Dad adds, "I'm telling you, the ads will write themselves. *Works like a sharm!* Or: *Sharm the pants off your floor with this space-saving tool!*"

"Third time's a sharm?" Mom adds.

"Lucky sharm?" I suggest.

Max is talking about his room, so I don't think he hears us. "I could probably fit all my shirts in the armoire without it, but…"

"You'll be the envy of everyone!" Dad says. "If people ask where you got it, let me know."

We hang up with Max, and the sounds in our house feel different, like everything is muted except scraping knives and the ticking clock on the wall. Our table feels off-balance too. I slide the bowl of lemons from the center toward Max's chair, but it doesn't help.

"I called Jacuzzi today to see when her next doctor appointment is, but she didn't answer," Mom says after a minute.

I concentrate on stabbing my salad with my fork. The program from the memorial service is still in my pocket. I should say I saw her, but I'm feeling a little guilty about confessing that I followed her and crashed a funeral.

"Maybe she was at the doctor when you called," Dad replies.

"I told her I could go with her. I hope she didn't drive herself."

"I'm sure she didn't. She probably took the bus."

Dad switches the topic, and it feels like my moment to say something about Jacuzzi has passed.

After dinner, it's my turn to load the dishwasher. When I'm sure my parents aren't around, I take the program out of my pocket and unfold it.

"I hope you had a good life, George," I say to the man's photo. "Sorry we crashed your funeral. Your grandkids are really sweet."

Inside the program is an obituary. I don't think I've read one before, and it occurs to me that obituaries could be a good source of inspiration for characters in my movies, so I skim it.

No offense to George, but the obituary could have used a few more details and interesting anecdotes. Like his childhood, for example. All it says is "He grew up in San Diego." So that tells me something, but what was he like as a kid? The only hobby mentioned is fishing. Surely in his eighty-four years, he did more things for fun than fish. At the very least, he probably had some good fishing stories. Whoever wrote this could have included one of those.

The last paragraph is a list of his surviving family members. I'm about to skip the list of names and put the paper in the recycling bin when this phrase jumps out at me: *George is survived by his devoted wife of fifty-three years, Annette Winthrop.*

Annette Winthrop? *Annette* Winthrop?

As in "Happy 10th birthday" Annette? "Thank you for a million things" Annette?

That Annette? I don't know any other person named Annette. It might be a crazy leap, but between the inscription with my grandmother's name and Annette's, and Jacuzzi going to the memorial for the husband of a woman named Annette...Maybe all the Nancy Drew books I've been reading are getting to me. Still, I have an itchy feeling this is more than a coincidence.

The program has photos of George over the years, including his wedding photo. I run to my room and find the old photograph of Jacuzzi tucked inside the Nancy Drew book. I compare Annette Winthrop to the three women in the 1993 photo, and there is no mistaking it: One of the women—the one who looks about the same age as Jacuzzi—is definitely Annette Winthrop, wife of George for fifty-three years.

That night as I work on my homework, I'm a little distracted. One part of my brain is solving math problems, but another part is stuck on the mystery of the old Nancy Drew books. I keep running through what I know:

The books showed up at Mom's store.

There was a photo of Jacuzzi and two other women in the box.

But Jacuzzi said it's not her.

There was an old message in one of the books to "Annette" from "Susie."

Jacuzzi's real name is Susie.

But Jacuzzi said the Susie who wrote in the book is not her.

And she didn't know anyone named Annette.

But she went to a memorial service for someone whose wife is named Annette.

Something strange is going on here, and I want to get to the bottom of it.

13

The Real Carolyn Keene

AT SCHOOL THE NEXT DAY, I CAN'T WAIT TO SHOW THE MEMORIAL program to Nell and Cam in Mr. Orson's class. But as soon as we pull our desks together, Cam holds up the book she checked out from the library and says, "You'll never guess what I learned about the history of Nancy Drew. There's so much good stuff in here!"

I'm restless to share my Annette discovery, but as a screenwriter, I can also appreciate the art of saving a reveal for the end of a scene, so I keep quiet and listen to Cam.

"Get this: There was this guy—Edward Stratemeyer—and he was alive a long time ago. Like more than a hundred years ago. And he loved to read and write adventurous, fast-paced stories. He was getting a lot of his books published, but he had so many ideas, way more than he could write himself, so in 1905 he started a company called the Stratemeyer Syndicate. Edward came up with the ideas and outlined the plots, and then he hired other writers to write most of the books. He also made up an author name for each series—a pen name. Readers didn't know the authors weren't real people, and many series had several people writing under the same pen name."

My knees bounce as I wait not so patiently for Cam to get to Nancy Drew.

"At one point," Cam continues, "Edward had something like thirty different series going at once, each with a new book out every year."

"Thirty?" Nell repeated.

"Yep. Tom Swift, the Bobbsey Twins, Honey Bunch, the Hardy Boys—"

Cam is ticking these series names off on her fingers, and I don't think it's important for us to hear every single one, so I cut her off.

"And Nancy Drew," I say, helping her get to the point.

"Yeah, but it took Edward a while to get to Nancy Drew. It wasn't until the late 1920s, after his series the Hardy Boys became popular, that he thought kids might be interested in a similar series but with a female detective. And that's when he came up with the idea for Nancy Drew."

"And he was right!" I say. "Nancy Drew went on to be a big hit. That's a great story—"

I'm reaching for the memorial service program in my backpack when Cam says, "But wait, there's more!" My shoulders sag.

"So Edward wanted to create a series about a girl detective, and he hired this lady who wrote for another one of his series. Her name was Mildred Wirt Benson. Edward asked her, 'Can you write three mysteries superfast about a girl detective?' And Mildred said, 'No problem.' And he said, 'Make the detective daring and smart.' And Mildred was like, 'Hi, I'm the first student to graduate from the University of Iowa graduate program in journalism. Also, I was a competitive swimmer. I've got this, dude.'

"So, she wrote the first three Nancy Drew books and sent them in, and he loved them, and all three were published in 1930."

"And the rest is history!" I interject. "What a happy end—"

"It's actually not a happy ending," Cam says.

"It's not?" I sink back in my seat.

"Edward died two weeks after the first three books were published."

Nell claps her hands to her mouth. "Oh no!"

"Oh brother." Despite myself, I feel bad for Edward. He had no clue how popular Nancy Drew would become.

"His daughters inherited the Stratemeyer Syndicate, but they didn't know how to run a publishing company. They tried to sell it, but this was also at the beginning of the Great Depression, and it was horrible timing. So Edward's daughters figured out how to keep the business going, and they asked Mildred to write more Nancy Drew titles, and she ended up writing twenty-three of the first thirty books."

"And then what happened?" Nell asked.

"I don't know, that's as far as I got in the book."

Cam's story ends with a fizzle, but that's okay, because I've got my discovery to reveal. I clear my throat and say, "I've got something to share too."

I whip out the program from George Winthrop's funeral, as well as the 1993 photograph that had been left in the box with the Nancy Drew books.

"Remember the inscription from Susie to Annette in *The Message in the Hollow Oak*?"

I open the program to show the obituary. "I found Annette!"

Nell's jaw drops as she reads the name. But Cam barely looks at the program. She's fixated on the 1993 photo. She smacks a hand on the table and shouts, "No way!" Which, to be honest, feels a little over-the-top, even though I was going for the shock factor.

Cam taps the older lady standing in the middle of the picture, not young Jacuzzi or young Annette Winthrop.

"That's Mildred Wirt Benson!" she says. "The original Carolyn Keene!"

"What?!" I ask.

"Your grandmother—or her evil twin—is standing with Mildred Wirt Benson! I recognize her from the book I'm reading—there are a bunch of pictures of her in it," Cam explains.

Nell and I lean closer to the photo.

"That's really her?" Nell asks.

Last weekend, when I first found the photo in the box, I looked up the photo's date combined with Jacuzzi's name and found nothing. But what happens if I use "Mildred Wirt Benson" as a search term?

"Hold on." I jump up and retrieve a laptop from the class cart. After it powers on, I do a search for "1993 Mildred Wirt Benson."

Right away it's obvious we're onto something. I read aloud from the first entry:

"'In April 1993, the University of Iowa made international headlines when it hosted a scholarly conference about Nancy Drew—'"

The three of us look at one another, eyes wide.

"Your grandmother went to a Nancy Drew conference!" Cam says.

"With Annette Winthrop," I add.

"And they met the original Carolyn Keene!" Nell says.

We read more and learn that the conference was a pretty big deal. It was organized to honor the legacy of Nancy Drew, which hadn't been done before. In fact, this convention was the first time Mildred Wirt Benson was widely recognized as the original Carolyn Keene.

"She didn't get recognized for creating Nancy Drew until she was *eighty-seven* years old?!" Cam exclaims. "Can you imagine that?"

I'm not sure I can. How would it feel to have a major role in creating an iconic character, one who's known for decades and by generations and has TV shows and movies made about them, and nobody knows you had anything to do with it?

"Look at this." Nell points to the screen. "At one point in time, one of Edward Stratemeyer's daughters said she was the real Carolyn Keene and created Nancy Drew. And because of that, there are still people who think she did, even though the truth is widely known now."

Just the other day, I was annoyed when Ben didn't tell Mr. Orson I was the one who came up with the Shellfish Holmes idea. Writing twenty-three novels and having someone else take credit for all that work? That seems unbearable.

"Mildred Wirt Benson sounds great," Cam says, bringing my attention back to the computer screen. The article talks about how a female main character like Nancy Drew, who was independent and bold and held her own with the male characters, always outsmarting the criminal ones, was uncommon in 1930, when the books were first published. "I love this quote." Cam points to words from Mildred Wirt Benson about creating Nancy Drew: "'I just naturally thought that girls could do the things boys did.'"

We're so into our research, we don't realize Mr. Orson has stopped by to check on us. "You three seem to be enjoying yourselves!" Today his shirt reads, "Hyperbole: Best. Thing. Ever."

"We're finding lots of information for our documentary," Cam says.

As she shares some of what we've learned, my attention is drawn across the room to the howling laughs and groans of Ben and Link. Nobody is alarmed by these noises, because we've been hearing them throughout group work. Isabelle's project is now called *Sherlock Nose: The Big Stink*. It's no longer the story of a lobster detective. Instead, it's about a detective with a fantastic sense of smell that helps him solve mysteries, and his archnemesis, who tries to thwart him with stinkier and stinkier weapons. Apparently, Ben and Link aren't satisfied using their imagination and had to bring in a collection of disgusting-smelling objects—sweaty socks, a thermos of spoiled milk, a container with fruit so old it's growing mold—and they're taking turns smelling and debating which to use in their movie. Isabelle has been inspecting the ends of her hair instead of weighing in on which item is the grossest.

"And what's the main idea for your project?" Mr. Orson asks us, pulling me back to our Nancy Drew group.

"We're exploring why Nancy Drew has lasted for almost one hundred years," Nell answers.

"Interesting, interesting." Mr. Orson nods. "And you're collecting information by..."

"Reading about the history of the series, researching different covers over time to compare how Nancy Drew has changed," Cam says.

"And we're meeting with a Larksville College professor tomorrow," I say.

"A scholar's perspective is great. Will you include more interviews?"

The three of us look at one another, considering Mr. Orson's question.

"We could interview a bookseller. I know that Maureen at Turn the Page read the books when she was younger. She could talk about that and selling them today," I suggest.

"Hey, what about your grandmother?" Cam says. "She met the original Carolyn Keene! We should totally include her."

"Oh...yeah, that would be good, wouldn't it?" I'm not sure why I feel hesitant about the idea. Cam's right—it would be great to interview her. But if Jacuzzi didn't say anything about the conference when I first showed her that photo, then she might not want to talk about it for our documentary either. Nell's already adding Jacuzzi to our list, and having her be a part of the documentary *is* a good idea, so I don't say anything.

"Anyone else?" Mr. Orson asks.

"We know a cranky librarian who isn't a fan of the series...," Cam throws out.

I think Cam is making a joke, but Mr. Orson nods. "Showing another side to Nancy Drew and how a character can endure over time, even if they aren't embraced by everyone, seems like a terrific idea. Especially from a librarian's perspective. I like that! Keep up the good work!" Mr. Orson says, and moves on to another group.

As we continue to talk and plan, I'm getting more and more excited. This project feels like it will be way better than my original *Shellfish Holmes* script would have been. If we can pull everything together the way we plan to, I think our Nancy Drew documentary has a pretty good chance of getting chosen for the screening at the Curio.

14

Meeting the Professor

THAT WEEKEND, NELL AND I RIDE OVER TO THE FOUNTAIN IN THE PARK, where Cam is waiting for us. Kelsey is supposed to be there too, but she's not. As we straddle our bikes and wait, looking in different directions to see if we spot her coming, irritation bubbles up. I still question her trustworthiness since the eraser incident at the bookstore.

"She's not coming," I finally say.

I'm about to suggest we head to Turn the Page to see if we can interview Maureen when Nell says, "Is that her?" She points to a bicyclist making their way down a path to us.

Kelsey waves as she approaches. "Maizy, hi!" After she comes to a stop next to us, she introduces herself to Nell and Cam.

"Sorry I'm late," Kelsey says. "I was volunteering at the animal shelter this morning, walking the sweetest little corgi mix, and he was afraid of everything! I ended up having to carry him back to the shelter, because I knew I'd never make it here in time otherwise. But then I felt bad about leaving him so abruptly, so I sat and gave him some cuddles first."

Kelsey's story sounds like the most made-up-for-sympathy excuse I've ever heard. I turn to Nell and Cam, expecting scowls and cynical looks, but instead their eyes shine like they've been hypnotized.

"Aww, that dog sounds so cute," Nell coos. "That's so cool that you volunteer at a shelter."

"My aunt has a corgi, and he's awesome," Cam adds.

"Well, if your aunt wants another, you can tell her there's a sweetheart named Yoshi at the Larksville Shelter. Want to see his picture?"

Kelsey pulls out her phone and shows us a brown-and-white dog with a dopey grin, and my irritation twists into guilt for being so suspicious of her. I guess she wasn't lying after all.

"He really is cute," I agree.

We pedal off to meet Professor Vale on the Larksville College campus with Kelsey leading the way. We lock our bikes next to a café, and I'm assuming we got there before the professor, because everyone sitting at the tables looks like a college student. But then a petite young woman stands and waves to Kelsey.

"Hi, Professor Vale!" Kelsey calls, and leads us over.

Professor Vale has a pixie cut and a nose ring and wears a T-shirt for a band called the Bangles. She offers her hand for each of us to shake in turn. "Wonderful to meet you girls!" She points to her cup of coffee and croissant. "You want to get a lemonade or anything first?"

We all say no and sit. Around us, people are studying with books and laptops, or debating topics that make no sense to me.

"So, you girls are doing a school project on Nancy Drew?" Professor Vale asks.

The three of us take turns explaining the documentary.

"The main question we're interested in is why Nancy Drew has remained popular for almost one hundred years," Nell sums up.

The professor nods and sips her coffee. "That's a terrific direction. What are your theories so far?"

"The original books are fast-paced and exciting and funny," I say.

"Funny?" the professor asks.

"Well, maybe not intentionally funny, but the way Nancy is able to do anything, no matter the situation, is funny to me. Like in the one I'm currently reading, she knows how to do these fancy competitive dives and wins a swimming contest."

"Ah, yes!" Professor Vale smiles widely. "Her perfection is a bit unrealistic."

"But somehow it doesn't ruin the book."

"Why do you think that is?" She leans forward, as if she's eager to hear my answer.

"Maybe..." I pause to think about this. "Maybe it's because everyone in the story agrees that Nancy is exceptional. It's almost like reading a book with dragons. When everyone in the story agrees there are dragons, you go with it, even though there aren't dragons in real life."

"I like that!" Kelsey says.

Professor Vale nods. "Me too."

"We also think Nancy Drew has been around for so long because she was doing things that weren't typical of women in the time she was first written, and so she's been a role model," Cam says. "Like the woman who created her." She shares what we learned about Mildred Wirt Benson.

"You girls are doing great research. I love what you've come up with so far," Professor Vale says. "There is some additional history I think you should consider, although it might be difficult to hear. But it's important to know that not all of Nancy Drew's past is glamorous and positive."

We exchange looks. "Okay," we say a little uneasily, as we don't know what we're agreeing to hear.

"Can we record this? In case we want to use it in our documentary?" I ask.

"Sure," Professor Vale says.

I set up my camera and tripod, making adjustments until I'm satisfied with how the frame looks. Nell flips open her notebook to take notes. Cam looks to see if I'm ready, and I give a thumbs-up.

"Let's hear it," Cam says.

Professor Vale clears her throat. "As you said, Nancy Drew has inspired many readers over the years. And I think you're smart to note that it's not her character alone that makes for a successful formula. It's her character combined with a compelling storytelling package. Page-turning mysteries.

"But to really understand Nancy Drew and her longevity, it's good to consider all aspects of her history, how she's changed over time, and, most important, *why* she changed.

"The first iteration of the series, from the 1930s to the 1950s, had some shameful racist content. When characters of color were introduced, they were often presented as suspicious or unintelligent or some other unfavorable representation. And Nancy herself is downright awful in some of those books, in the way she treats these characters. In the day and age those stories were written, portrayals like that were unfortunately common. But just because something is common doesn't mean it's acceptable."

The three of us shift in our seats and dart looks at one another. I don't know what Nell and Cam are thinking, but I was enjoying reading the books, and now I'm not sure how I should feel about that. I don't remember noticing anything offensive. Maybe I haven't read the books with the racist content.

Professor Vale continues. "In 1959, the publisher decided to revise all the Nancy Drew books that had been published to date, and in these revisions, they removed what they understood to be racist. Some of the revised versions have completely different plots because they decided not to work with what had been previously written."

"Well, that's good, right?" Nell asked. "They fixed the problem?"

Professor Vale tilts her head, considering her words. "They addressed concerns that had been raised, which is good, but I wouldn't say they fixed the problem. And I wish I could say those revisions were motivated purely out of compassion for readers who were rightly offended by the stereotyping and to correct old wrongs. However, editing out the racism wasn't the primary concern. What prompted the revisions in the first place was money. They wanted to make the books shorter so they'd cost less to produce, and so they decided to address the racism at the same time. In fact, you can tell if you have an original version of a Nancy Drew title if there are twenty-five chapters. The revised editions have twenty."

"The ones left at my mom's store must have twenty-five chapters, then." I didn't notice that they all had the same number of chapters, but I know the ones I read were published before 1959.

"And the books that belonged to my mom have twenty," Nell says. "I'm reading one with my younger brother, and last night we finished chapter eighteen. He wanted to keep reading because we're so close to the end, but it was already way past his bedtime."

"Yellow-spined hardbacks?" Professor Vale asks.

"Yes," Nell says.

Professor Vale nods. "The first thirty or so with that design are revised versions of the original mysteries published before 1959."

She continues. "The other important reason why I wouldn't say the revisions fixed the problem is because of how the publisher dealt with the racist content. 'Removing it' to them meant removing any reference to a character of color. So you have Nancy, whose blond hair and blue eyes are often called out and praised. And no references to other cultures, races, or any diversity, which is essentially racism dressed in different clothes."

We must look a bit stunned or disappointed to hear this, because Professor Vale stops talking for a minute and gives us an apologetic smile. "I feel like I might be tearing down heroes, and that's not what I'm trying to do. Nancy Drew is still worth your admiration and a deserving subject for your documentary. All of us here, all five of us women at this table, are able to do the things we do, say the things we say, wear the things we wear, study the things we study, because of the women who came before us. Nancy

Drew inspired girls in the 1930s, and she continues to inspire people today. That's pretty exceptional."

I remember how Maureen had said reading Nancy Drew helped her believe in herself and think it was possible for her to own a bookstore one day.

I share this with Professor Vale and she nods. "Exactly. I'm not sure I can think of another female character in popular culture who's had the same presence and impact. But I think it's important to acknowledge her complete history as you answer your question, because if the publisher hadn't addressed the racist content in 1959, then I'm not convinced Nancy Drew would still be a household name today. They were willing to retell her story and recast her character in different ways—beginning with the revised version of the originals, and then again and again with every new variation of a Nancy Drew series or show or movie that has been produced since. They've let her grow and change, just like we do in real life. Right? As Maya Angelou said, we learn better, we do better."

"So maybe," Nell ventures, "the reason why Nancy Drew has lasted for one hundred years is because she represents an idea? And enough readers still like that idea, and so she continues to be relevant?"

Professor Vale snaps her fingers. "Yes! And what's the idea? What could she represent?"

"That women...can be smart and independent and brave," Nell replies.

"That they can do anything a man does," Cam says, referencing the quote she liked from Mildred Wirt Benson.

Professor Vale nods. "Think about superhero stories. Spider-Man, Batman...how popular are they? Incredibly popular, right? They represent ideas people can latch on to: A regular person can have a secret and amazing side to them. Good triumphs over evil. But we don't have just one Batman story or characterization that we hear over and over, or one Spider-Man story. Their stories endure because they continue to be told in new ways, keeping enough of what's familiar, but modernizing or giving a little twist to what's been done before."

After our meeting with Professor Vale, Kelsey rides with us back through campus to the edge of the park. We thank her and ride on.

"Professor Vale and Kelsey are both so nice," Nell gushes as we pedal.

"It was cool of Kelsey to help us out and arrange a meeting," Cam agrees.

I can't argue with that, but something is still not sitting right with me.

"Don't you wonder why, though? Like, what's in it for her?" I ask.

My question hangs in the air with only the whir of our wheels turning until Cam asks, "Well, are *you* only nice if you want something?"

"Of course not," I say, feeling dumb for having asked in the first place. I do nice things because it feels good, or I'm interested in helping someone, or it simply seems like what should be done. "You're right, Cam."

I was hung up on why I couldn't be more trusting of Kelsey until Cam turned my question around on me. I wonder if it has to do with Izzy, and how she's been so hot and cold with me lately. Maybe that's messing with my ability to tell if someone's being sincere or phony.

I continue to think about this as we pedal, and Professor Vale's words come back to me. She said some things endure because people are committed to retelling the story. Izzy and I don't feel like we're "enduring," and I haven't understood why.

But maybe what's happened is Izzy stopped wanting to tell our story. Maybe she's trying to tell a different one now.

15

Hidden Gems

AFTER MEETING WITH PROFESSOR VALE, THE THREE OF US GO TO THE bookstore and the library and record short conversations with Maureen and Mr. Noys about Nancy Drew. We've got so much material to work with now. Before the three of us part ways, Cam says, "You'll interview your grandmother too, right? That's all we have left on our list."

I hesitate for the briefest second before replying. "Yep!"

"This is going to be so good!" Nell says.

We say goodbye and split in three different directions: Cam heads to her house, Nell sets out for the rec center to watch her little brother's soccer game, and I start for home.

I should go to Jacuzzi's house now, but I don't. I know Cam and Nell are excited to include someone who met the original Carolyn Keene in our documentary—I am too. But I don't know how to ask Jacuzzi about the conference or the photo without it sounding like I'm accusing her of lying for not saying anything before.

I put off talking to Jacuzzi over the weekend. On Monday, I tell Nell and Cam she was busy, but I promise I'll talk to her soon.

And I'm going to.

I really am.

After school, I pack up my camera and tripod with the intention of going to Jacuzzi's house. I'm sitting on my bed, giving myself a pep talk, when my phone dings. It's a message from Max.

> How are things?

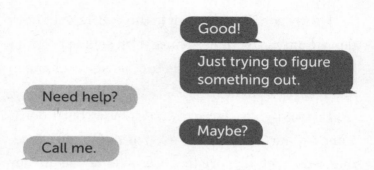

On the phone, I tell Max about following Jacuzzi to the funeral, and how I think she might have lied about not recognizing the photo or inscription in the Nancy Drew book, and how Nell and Cam and I figured out she'd once met the original Carolyn Keene.

"So we want to interview her for our project, but I'm worried she'll be mad if I ask her again about these things," I say.

"Jacuzzi won't get mad at you for being curious about her life," Max reassures me. "And just because you ask doesn't mean she has to answer. Bring her the photo and tell her what you learned. Stick to facts, not emotions. She might talk to you—you won't know until you ask. If she doesn't want to talk, it has nothing to do with you. Okay?"

"Okay."

My brother's advice makes sense, and it feels good to have a plan.

"Thanks, Max."

Things might have changed with Max off at college, but I'm glad we're still part of the same story.

⌒⌒⌒

Jacuzzi is out front, wearing a floppy hat and the baggy overalls that she, Max, and I decorated with our handprints when I was in kindergarten. She's pacing up and down her garden beds with a paper bag in one hand and some kind of tool in the other.

"Maizy! What a nice surprise! I'm looking for gems. Want to help?"

I open my mouth to reply, but I'm at a loss for words. Looking for gems in your front yard doesn't seem very...normal. Could she have fallen off her bike after the funeral the other day? She's moving fine in her walking boot, but maybe she hit her head. My stomach twists with guilt that I didn't stay at the park to follow her home.

But then Jacuzzi points near a shrub and says, "Found one!"

And sure enough, there's a gem on the ground.

"Huh," I say. "I didn't think they'd be real."

Jacuzzi crouches down and taps it with a fingernail. "It's plastic. Glued on a stick that's buried in the ground. In the spring, when my tulips and daffodils are blooming, I bury these where I want to see more flowers. Then I look for them in the fall, and I know where to plant new bulbs. For years, I always thought I'd remember, but the yard looks so different now compared to when the bulbs bloomed in early spring."

I watch Jacuzzi swipe back the wood-chip mulch, pull the gem out of the ground, and shove the cylinder-shaped tool in. It's some sort of mini shovel that she uses to scoop out dirt and make a hole. She drops one of the bulbs from her bag into the hole, fills it back up, and swipes the wood-chip mulch back over the top. It looks the same as before. If I hadn't been standing here watching, I'd never know there was something hidden underground.

Jacuzzi stands and brushes dirt from her knees. "There are more to be found," she says.

I'm so relieved she really is on a treasure hunt of sorts, I eagerly start searching along the border, peering under shrubs, lifting up the edges of plants that spread along the ground.

"Here's one!" I point to a gem next to a leafy mound blooming with burgundy flowers.

"Oh, goodie." Jacuzzi crosses over and begins to dig another hole.

When we're on our fifth bulb, I clear my throat. "So...you know how I'm doing the school project on Nancy Drew?"

Jacuzzi nods and keeps digging.

"My friends and I were hoping we could interview you."

"Me? Why?"

"Because you collected the books and have been a longtime fan, and also—" I clear my throat again. "We've done a lot of research about the Nancy Drew books, and remember that photo I found in the box that was left at Mom's store?

Jacuzzi stops digging for the briefest moment, then continues. "Yes, I remember."

"We learned that the older woman was Mildred Wirt Benson, who was the original Carolyn Keene, and the photo was taken at a Nancy Drew conference in 1993."

Jacuzzi wipes sweat off her brow.

"I'll understand if there's a reason you don't want to talk about it, but my friends and I were really excited that you might have met the original Carolyn Keene. And we were hoping you could share about it in our project. But only if you want.

"If that was you in the photo," I add, even though I'm pretty sure it was. I want Jacuzzi to feel like she can stick to the story she's been telling—or not telling—if that's what she's more comfortable with.

Jacuzzi holds her floppy hat back like she wants to make sure to really see me. Wind dances through her yard, carrying a handful of leaves. I can't tell from her expression what she's thinking or feeling. She doesn't look mad. She looks like she's listening. And considering.

"Let's go inside and have some cocoa and talk," she finally says.

I follow her inside. Jacuzzi washes her hands, then takes out two mugs, pouring milk into each. As they heat in the microwave she says, "Meeting Mildred Wirt Benson was the highlight of that weekend. She was a smart woman. Exactly as I imagined Carolyn Keene would be. I went to that conference with a dear friend, and we were both so excited to meet her."

"Why didn't you say anything when I showed you the photo?"

The microwave dings, and Jacuzzi removes our mugs. She takes a deep breath before setting them on the counter. "Well, I froze, I guess. The photo took me by surprise. The photo itself was a good memory, but it was one good memory from a very difficult year. Seeing it like that, out of the blue, and with your mother there…I just panicked and didn't want to talk about it.

"Mom? Why did it matter that she was there?"

Jacuzzi stirs in the cocoa. Either she's concentrating hard on mixing it up well, or she's debating what to say next.

"That was the year I divorced your grandfather. That wasn't an easy decision to make, but it was the right one for me and your mother. Your grandfather was a big dreamer, but he was also reckless with our money. And that caused a lot of stress and instability. For years I hoped he would change and things would get better. And they would for a stretch, and I'd think *finally* we're on a good track. But then there'd be a new opportunity he couldn't pass up, and it was going to be the answer to all of our problems. There was always a hitch—he needed to quit his job or take out a loan, or we needed to move. But it would be worth it, so I shouldn't worry. If I asked questions or resisted, then I wasn't being supportive. And the opportunities never lived up to their promise. We were stuck in a cycle that I feared would never get broken, unless I was the one to break it."

I can imagine how this would be hard, but I'm still not sure what it has to do with the Nancy Drew conference, until Jacuzzi continues. "When I was away at that conference, I decided this time I'd go through with asking for a divorce. And when I got home, I did. Once I made the decision, I knew it was the right thing to do, for me and your mom. Your mom, of course, was very upset. She didn't see things the way I did, which must be why my knee-jerk reaction the other day was to clam up when I saw that photo. That and…"

I sip my cocoa, waiting for her to finish her sentence. When she doesn't, I ask, "And?"

"Well, you know, the unexpectedness of it all. Why that photo would turn up at your mom's store like that."

"Is Annette the other woman in the photo?"

If my question surprises Jacuzzi, she doesn't show it. She sips from her mug and nods. "She was my childhood best friend. We did everything together, just like you and Izzy."

I flinch at this, but I don't think Jacuzzi notices. She doesn't know things are different between us right now.

"Annette and I, our common bond was always Nancy Drew. Even as we got older and went to different schools and headed down different paths in life, we remained friends. We wrote each other letters and shared thoughts about the latest titles we were reading. We traded books back and forth. We'd go thrifting and look for Nancy Drew books to add to our collections."

"So she left the box of books, then, right?"

"I don't know," Jacuzzi replies.

"You didn't ask her?"

"I haven't spoken to Annette in years. Since that conference, in fact."

My mouth hangs open. A million thoughts are running through my head, and the one leading the pack is that I know Jacuzzi went to Annette's husband's memorial. And wouldn't she have talked to Annette then? I don't want to explain how I know about all that, so instead what I say is, "But she was your best friend!"

Those words shift something within me. Something small but pesky, like a thistle stuck in my sock. *A best friend shouldn't just stop being a best friend* is what I'm thinking.

"What happened?" I ask.

"This will sound silly, but we had an argument about the character Ned in the Nancy Drew books, of all things. She thought Nancy and Ned were a great couple; I thought Nancy didn't need Ned. He seemed like a lump to me."

Jacuzzi starts wiping her counter with a rag as she talks, sweeping invisible crumbs into her hand and shaking them into the sink.

"But our argument about Ned wasn't really about Ned. You see, I told Annette I had decided to get a divorce as soon as I got home from the conference, and she didn't think it was a good idea. She worried about how I would support myself. She didn't think it would set a good example for your mom. I was more worried about the example I'd already been setting for years by *not* doing anything."

I'm trying to picture this—Jacuzzi when she was my mom's age arguing with a friend to the point of not talking. Like me and Izzy.

"And then after I went through with the divorce, Annette just disappeared."

"She disappeared?"

"Not literally. And maybe it happened gradually, but the change felt immediate to me."

She rinses the rag under the faucet and squeezes water out.

"When you showed me that photo," Jacuzzi says, "my first thought was Annette must have left the books. I looked her up online and, sadly, found an obituary for her husband. Apparently, he'd been very ill and passed away earlier this year. His memorial was last week."

"Oh really?" I say as casually as I can manage. "That is sad."

"The timing of the books showing up and the memorial—I thought that must be significant. Maybe Annette was trying to communicate something to me. I went to pay my respects to George and hoped to talk to Annette too. But I left before she even saw me."

I'm concentrating so hard on acting like I don't already know this that I almost miss the last part of what she said.

"You left? Why?"

"It was too much for me. Too many emotions unexpressed for thirty years. And then I started to think I was wrong—maybe she hadn't left those books. I didn't want my presence at the memorial to make an already difficult day even worse."

"But how else can you explain the books? She must have been the one to leave them."

"Maybe. But I've lived in this house for a long time, Maizy. Annette knows where to find me. If she wanted to give me those books, she wouldn't have needed to leave them at your mom's store. She might not even know my daughter owns Alter Ego. She might have been genuinely donating them. I'm afraid that friendship is very much in my past."

I don't know why I'm so unwilling to accept this. I know thirty years is a long time not to speak with someone, but if they really were such good friends at one time…It makes me think of how easily Nell and I picked up our friendship again. Of course, for us it was three years, not thirty, but we've only been alive for almost twelve. Three years is a fourth of our life so far.

Jacuzzi and her old best friend need each other. I'm determined to bring them back together, and I think I have an idea how.

16

Get a Clue, Maizy Drew

"YOU WANT TO DO WHAT?!" CAM SAYS.

"Are you sure that's a good idea?" Nell adds.

We're in Mr. Orson's class the next day, and I've just caught them up on my conversation with Jacuzzi and showed the clips from the interview she let me record after we talked.

"Finding Annette is a great idea," I insist. "I did an internet search last night and located two addresses for a George and Annette Winthrop in Larksville."

"And you're wanting to do this for our project?" Cam asks.

"No, for Jacuzzi."

"But, Maizy—" Nell taps her pencil on her notebook. "Isn't this meddling? If Jacuzzi wants to reconnect with her friend, she'll do it on her own."

"But that's the thing—I don't think she can. I mean, I know she *can*, but..."

I try to find the words to describe what my intuition is telling me. A hunch, as Nancy Drew would say.

"I think Jacuzzi misses her friend but she's worried about putting herself out there. And I think Annette feels the same way. That's why she left the books. Leaving the books was a safe way to put herself out there."

"*If* she left the books," Cam says.

"Annette left the books," I insist. "I refuse to believe it was a coincidence, and who else would leave them?"

Cam opens her mouth, but I cut her off before she can say it. "It wasn't an evil twin!"

Nell turns to Cam. "Does Link know about this fixation with evil twins? Should he be worried?"

"Look," I continue, "if Nancy Drew has taught me anything, it's that meddling solves other people's problems."

Cam scrunches her nose. "I'm not sure that's right."

"People are always thanking her for getting involved," I insist. "Without Nancy's meddling, think of the kidnapped people and hidden wills and stolen jewels that would never be found!"

"Did I miss something?" Nell asks. "I thought we were talking about Jacuzzi and an old friend, not capturing crooks and thieves."

"Besides," I continue, "is it really meddling if Annette was the one to leave the books in the first place? If her books were a message, all I'm doing is trying to reply. It's almost *rude* not to try to find her."

They both roll their eyes. "Okay, what are you going to say if you find her?" Cam asks.

"I'm not sure. But if she left the books, I probably won't have to say much at all."

"For the record, I think this is a bad idea," Nell says. "But I'll help you if you're sure you want to do this."

"I second that," Cam agrees. "I have a feeling you're going to do it anyway, so we might as well go along with you."

We make a plan to visit the two addresses for Annette Winthrop after school. Then we review our documentary so far on our group laptop. We've already recorded the reenactment of me finding the box and inserted clips from some of the interviews, as well as a voice-over narration of the history of Nancy Drew. We pick a place to insert clips from Jacuzzi's interview, which I can add in later tonight. The project is pretty good, but...

"It's missing something," Cam says.

"I agree." I can't quite put my finger on what. We've got the history covered, and the script I wrote narrates the story in a compelling way, if I do say so myself. But...

"Maybe it's too serious?" Nell suggests.

"The factual parts are what make it so interest-ing, though," Cam says.

"Maybe there's a way we can add in something fun, like a recurring bit. Maybe we break it up with trivia questions?" I suggest.

"Trivia's still on the serious side," Cam argues. "It feels like a quiz."

"You know what might be fun?" Nell says. "What if we make up a Nancy Drew quiz and then do random on-the-street interviews? We might get a variety of responses that include people who've never heard of her and longtime fans."

"Yes!" I say. "That's what's missing. It's not coming across how Nancy Drew has been beloved for so long. I mean, we say that in the documentary, but there's a difference between hearing the words and *feeling* them. It's the feeling part that's missing."

"What if we set up a Nancy Drew booth at the library's used-book sale this weekend?" Cam suggests. "It'll be held at the park, and there's bound to be a lot of booklovers there. We could spend an hour quizzing people, and then we'd still have Sunday to edit in the new material and finalize the video."

We all love this idea.

"We should display your collection of books," Nell says. "Finding that box is what starts off the documentary, and maybe they'll draw people's attention. We might hear some interesting memories from people if they have a chance to page through them."

As Nell is talking, I realize this new plan could work perfectly with my other plan to reunite Annette and Jacuzzi. I pull the laptop to me, open a blank file, and start typing: *Do you love Nancy Drew?*

"What are you doing?" Cam asks.

"I'm making a flyer for us to take this afternoon when we look for Annette. If the address we go to isn't where she lives, then we'll just be kids going door-to-door for a school project. And if we *do* find her, then maybe I can get her and Jacuzzi to come to the booth at the same time for a reunion."

Cam and Nell exchange a look but don't say anything. There's a photo saved on our group laptop of my Nancy Drew collection that we used in the documentary, so I insert that in the flyer, skim the text one more time, and press print.

We get to work on the quiz next, deciding it should be a mix of trivia about the characters and

DO
YOU LOVE
NANCY DREW?
Stop by our table at the
LARKSVILLE LIBRARY
~used-book sale~
Saturday, LARKSVILLE PARK

plots, and also the history and fashion facts Cam and Nell have been researching.

"I've got one," I say. "In *The Message in the Hollow Oak*, Bess sleepwalks in her hotel room and is in danger of falling off a balcony. What does Nancy do? (A) Pulls her back, (B) Pushes a trampoline underneath the balcony, (C) Ropes her with a lasso, or (D) Freaks out and does nothing."

"The answer has got to be *pulls her back*, right?" Cam asks.

"It's definitely not *freaks out and does nothing*," Nell adds. "That doesn't sound like Nancy Drew at all."

"She *ropes her with a lasso*," I say.

"What?!" Nell shrieks, and Cam laughs.

"Nancy knows how to throw a lasso?" Cam says.

"Of course! She's Nancy Drew!"

"And *why* was there a lasso in the hotel room?" Nell asks.

We are laughing, and I'm feeling happy and excited about our project, but something draws my attention across the room to Isabelle. She looks away when she sees me, but not before her unhappy expression pricks a tiny hole in my enthusiasm.

HOW WELL DO YOU KNOW NANCY DREW?

1. In *The Message in the Hollow Oak*, Bess sleepwalks in her hotel room and is in danger of falling off a balcony. What does Nancy do?

   A) Pulls her back to safety.

   B) Pushes a trampoline underneath the balcony.

   C) Ropes her with a lasso.

   D) Freaks out and does nothing.

2. Which of the following names was originally assigned to the famous girl sleuth before the books were actually written?

   A) Stella Strong

   B) Leona Lion

   C) Anita Mystery

   D) Madeline Clue

3. What accessory does Nancy hold in her iconic silhouette?

   A) Flashlight

   B) Notebook

   C) Magnifying glass

   D) Pencil

4. What is Nancy's dad's occupation?
   A) Doctor
   B) Teacher
   C) Detective
   D) Lawyer

5. Who is Carolyn Keene?
   A) Mildred Wirt Benson
   B) Walter Karig
   C) Harriet Stratemeyer Adams
   D) All of the above

17

Looking for Annette

AFTER SCHOOL, WE STOP OUR BIKES IN FRONT OF THE FIRST ADDRESS I wrote down for George and Annette Winthrop. The house looks like it's been frozen in time for forty years, with beige stucco and a blank expanse of lawn that's faded to yellow green. Hedges run under the front windows, and the shades are drawn. Other than chalk drawings on the sidewalk and driveway, it's a tidy but bland front yard.

We've rehearsed what to say in the event a random not-Annette person lives here—we'll simply act as if we're going door-to-door and hand the person our flyer and invite them to stop by the Nancy Drew booth. And if Annette herself answers, I'll explain I found her books and we'll arrange a time for her and Jacuzzi to meet. Instant friend reunion.

Nell has the flyer for our Nancy Drew booth in hand.

"Are you sure you want to do this?" she asks.

"She might not be home," I reply.

"Only one way to find out." Cam drops her bike on the grass. Nell and I do too, and then the three of us walk up to the front porch.

I ring the doorbell and we hear a tambourine and running footsteps, but nobody answers.

We ring the bell again.

The doorknob begins to turn at the same time there's a distant yell: "Do not answer that! Do you hear me?!"

I step back, bumping into Cam and Nell. "Do we have the wrong house?" But the house numbers over the door match the address I wrote down.

Now it's silent on the other side of the door.

"Maybe we should go—" Nell says, but before she finishes her sentence, the door opens to reveal a woman a bit younger than my mom.

"Hi, is Annette home?" I ask. Somewhere in the back of the house, an electronic piano clangs the same note over and over and over.

"Sorry, you have the wrong house. Does your friend live at the green one down the street? There's a family with kids your age there."

The woman steps back, ready to close the door, when a little hand tugs on her pants. She turns and hoists up a small boy munching on a cracker. And not just any boy either, but Michael, the one we were accidental babysitters for at the playground last week.

"Ohhh…," Cam says in a low voice.

A little head pops out from behind the woman. It's Gabriella, and she's wearing gigantic green sunglasses.

If Annette is the grandmother of these kids, then this woman must be Annette's daughter or daughter-in-law. I was prepared for the possibility that this might be an old address for Annette, but not that someone else in her family might live here instead. Gabriella lowers her sunglasses to get a better look at us and says, "It's the Lava Girls!"

The mom boosts Michael higher on her hip. He's nibbling the perimeter of the cracker, turning it round and round as he eats.

"The...lava?" she repeats, giving us a quizzical look.

I shrug in a *Beats me* kind of way. The piano is still repeating from somewhere out of our view, and the woman turns to yell, "Chloe! Can you stop with the piano?!"

The *clang, clang, clang* abruptly stops.

Then it starts up again but much softer. I imagine Chloe very gently pressing her key over and over again. Her mom stares up at the porch ceiling and draws in a deep breath. Michael looks up at the ceiling with her.

"Bye!" Gabriella says, and darts off.

Cam nudges me, and the lines I rehearsed for a not-Annette encounter pop out of my mouth: "We're doing a school project on Nancy Drew and will be having a booth at the library book fair this Saturday. There will be an old collection you can look through and a quiz—"

Nell offers the flyer, but then there's an incredible and lingering crash from the back of the house, like one big thing fell onto another big thing and something broke and something else is rolling, rolling, rolling. Chloe's still playing that piano through it all: *clang, clang, clang.*

"Gabriella Augustine! I said no more circus acts!"

To us she says, "Sorry, girls. This isn't a good time."

She plucks the flyer from Nell's hand and closes the door.

⌒⌒⌒

The second address for George and Annette Winthrop is in the wealthy part of Larksville. There aren't sidewalks, which seems bizarre to me. You'd think with all the money people have in this part of the town, they could afford sidewalks.

We ride past the property without even realizing it at first. It's just a split-rail fence with a wall of

shrubs so tall you can't see any house. We don't figure it out until we get to the next place, which looks
like the White House relocated beside a creek. The
street number on the mailbox at the end of the long,
tree-lined drive is a higher number than the one
we are looking for, so we circle back. That's when
I notice the simple gravel path tucked between an
opening in the shrubs.

We ride our bikes partway down the drive,
which curves behind the bushes. The road is soon
hidden from view, and ahead of us is a farmhouse
with a wraparound porch in the middle of lush green
lawns, enormous old trees, and chickens strutting
underneath in the shade. Standing here, it's hard to
believe Target is only ten minutes away on my bike.
This place is like someone plunked Farm World in
the middle of suburbia.

"Are we even allowed to be here?" Nell asks.

"That depends why you're here." A woman
stands up from the middle of a garden bed. I was so
focused on the house and the wandering chickens,
I didn't notice her among the big leafy plants. She
looks about Jacuzzi's age, and, like my grandmother,

she appears to be gardening. A surge of hope rises in me.

"Are you Annette Winthrop?" I ask.

"Yes." She high-steps over her plants, careful not to crush anything.

My hopeful feeling wobbles. What if I say the wrong thing?

A robot takes over my voice. "We're handing out these." I reach for the flyers in my basket while trying to maintain eye contact but miss the paper. I grasp at air and then awkwardly pet the flyer instead.

Nell gives me the *Are you okay?* side-eye.

Mrs. Winthrop peels off her gardening gloves as I'm taking in the lush borders full of different plants. Just like Jacuzzi's.

"Do you ever put gems in the ground?"

The question just pops out, like a burp, and now Cam is giving me the same look Nell did.

"Excuse me?" Mrs. Winthrop says.

I hurriedly explain. "When your tulips and daffodils bloom in the spring, you can stick gems where you want to see future flowers. Then in the fall, you find the gems and know where to plant your bulbs."

Mrs. Winthrop squints at us. "Who are you again?"

"We're Maizy, Cam, and Nell," I say, pointing to each of us in turn. "And…" I take a deep breath. "My mother owns Alter Ego."

Mrs. Winthrop frowns. "That's nice."

She doesn't seem to be connecting the dots, so I guess I need to spell it out. "My grandmother is Susie Anderson. I'm the one who found your box of Nancy Drew books and photo."

When I say Jacuzzi's name, Mrs. Winthrop's eyebrows rise, and that's when my hopeful nerves begin to plummet.

"You…you did leave the box, didn't you? There was this photo…" I pull off my backpack and unzip the pocket.

When Mrs. Winthrop looks at the photo, she presses two fingers to her lips. I can tell it's new to her. Well, maybe not brand-new, since she's in the photo, but I'm guessing it's been a while since she's seen it. Maybe even thirty years.

My face gets hot, and I suddenly wish I was anywhere but here. This was a stupid idea. How childish of me to think I could fix a thirty-year-old problem between adults with a little Nancy Drew meddling. I might as well have handed Mrs. Winthrop a piece of paper with *Do you want to be friends with Jacuzzi again? Check yes or no.*

When are you going to grow up, Maizy?

Those were Izzy's words, but now I'm saying them to myself.

Mrs. Winthrop clears her throat. "There's been some kind of mistake—"

But she doesn't need to keep talking. I've already yanked my bike around.

"I'm sorry to have bothered you!" I call back as I pedal away.

"Hold up, Maizy!" Cam calls. I hear gravel crunch under tires as she and Nell pedal after me.

"We're with you," Nell says.

We leave Mrs. Winthrop's neighborhood and ride along the path between the trees that leads into Larksville Park. We pass the clearing where Izzy and

I used to meet, and tears burn fiercely in the corners
of my eyes. I don't know if the tears come because
I was wrong about Annette, I'm embarrassed that
I tried to mend things for Jacuzzi, or I still feel sad
about Izzy.

We coast around the lake and Nell says, "Do you
want to talk about it?"

"Let's just focus on our documentary now, okay?"

"You got it," Cam says.

⁓

At home, I'm sprawled over my poufy chair, reading a new Nancy Drew. Actually, it's a very old
Nancy Drew, because it's *The Secret of the Old
Clock*, which is the first one ever. But it's new to
me. And I'm not so much reading as frowning at the
pages. I want to get carried away with Nancy and
this missing will she's trying to find, but my mind
keeps ping-ponging from Izzy to Jacuzzi to Annette
Winthrop...

Mom knocks on my door. "Can I come in?" she
asks.

"Sure."

I set my book on the floor. Mom peers at the cover. "Isn't that the first one?" she asks.

"Yep."

"Are you rereading it, or are you reading the books out of order?"

"I'm reading them out of order. I just go by whichever title sounds the most interesting when I start a new one."

"Huh." Mom sits on the edge of my bed. "I'd have to read them in order. I'd feel like I was breaking a rule if I didn't."

"What can I say? I'm a rebel."

Mom smiles. "I wanted to check in with you. It's been a big week for our family, with Max going off to college. I'm worried maybe I've been too caught up in my own stuff—you know, work and missing Max and worrying about Jacuzzi. I'd love to hear how you're doing."

"Me?" Honestly, I didn't even notice if Mom was busier than normal or preoccupied with thoughts about Max or Jacuzzi. I guess I was caught up in my own stuff too.

"I'm fine," I say.

"I saw you ride by Alter Ego this afternoon. You were by yourself, and that made me realize I haven't seen you and Izzy together lately. Is everything okay there?"

"I guess." I slide off the poufy chair and sit with my back against the bed. "Things are just different now. I don't really know why. It's like it changed overnight."

Mom hmmms an *I'm listening* sound.

"We were going to do that Shellfish Holmes project together for school, but there were, uhh… creative differences."

"So that's what prompted the Nancy Drew documentary?" Mom asks.

"That and the box of books." I stretch out my leg and tap a toe against the box, still next to my desk. "Hey, I interviewed Jacuzzi for my documentary," I say.

"You did?"

"Yeah, because I learned Jacuzzi met the woman who wrote the original Nancy Drew stories. That woman wrote this one I'm reading, actually."

"Jacuzzi met Carolyn Keene?" Mom says. "Huh, I'm not sure I knew that."

"The first Carolyn Keene," I clarify. "There've been a lot. Jacuzzi said they met the year she and Grandpa got divorced."

Mom clears her throat. "Oh, well. That might explain why I don't remember, then. Or didn't know. I was pretty mad at her that year. I'm not sure I would have cared even if she met Toad the Wet Sprocket."

I twist my neck to look up at Mom. "Who?"

She laughs and rumples my hair. "A favorite band when I was a teenager."

We're quiet for a minute. I'm thinking about Mom as a teenager, mad at her parents for getting divorced.

"Why do you think people stop wanting to tell a story?" I ask.

"What do you mean?"

"Well, like Jacuzzi and Grandpa. Getting a divorce is like they didn't want to continue the story of their marriage anymore."

"Hmm, I've never thought about it that way," Mom says. "I suppose you're right. But it's hard to say why people make decisions like that, at least in a general way. There are probably as many reasons to not tell a story as there are stories to tell.

"One thing I do know," Mom adds, "is that it hurts if you're part of the story someone doesn't want to tell anymore."

My eyes well up unexpectedly. I squeeze them shut, not wanting to cry.

"So, have you solved the mystery of who left those books?" Mom says this in a teasing voice—I don't think she realizes I actually *did* try to do that, or how close I thought I was to figuring it out. I'm grateful for the change in topic, though.

"No, but I'm having fun working with Cam and Nell. I like spending time with them."

It seems obvious now, but I didn't actually realize I felt that way until I said the words out loud. There is a twinge of guilt there too, that maybe I haven't tried as hard as I could to fix things with Izzy because I'm enjoying hanging out with Nell and Cam.

"Well, that's good to hear," Mom says. As if she senses my guilty twinge, she adds, "You know, it's normal for friendships to change and evolve over time. Of course, that doesn't mean it's easy. But it's nothing to feel terrible about, as long as you don't hurt the other person deliberately."

I rest my head against the bed, and she rumples my hair again.

"Thanks, Mom," I say.

18

A Lark in the Park

SATURDAY MORNING, I MEET NELL AND CAM AT ALTER EGO BEFORE THE
book fair. We're each going to dress up in different
Nancy Drew looks that Nell assigned us.

I'm 1930s Nancy Drew, based on the original
dust jacket of *The Secret of the Old Clock*. Nell made
me a blue cloche, like the one she wore to school,
and borrowed a button-up blazer from her mom. She
rummaged through the racks of Alter Ego and found
a blue skirt that we were able to pin and make fit.

Nell assigned herself the 1966 Nancy Drew from
the revised version of *The Secret of the Old Clock*.

Her hair is styled in a flip, and she's wearing a green dress with buttons down the front.

The problem we are having is Cam. First, she vetoed the red dress with a full skirt, à la the cover of *The Secret in the Old Attic*. The next option Nell suggests is a mustard-yellow turtleneck sweater to match the 1955 cover of *The Witch Tree Symbol*.

"No skirts, no dresses, no turtlenecks," Cam says.

"What about…" Nell is pacing the racks of costumes, studying them for inspiration. She begins to lift a boa when a black paw shoots out from underneath the clothes and smacks the feathers to the floor. Nell yelps and hops backward.

Cam crouches to lift the hanging clothes and reveals Marvin. Or at least his glowing green eyes and the tuft of white under his chin, since the dark space camouflages the rest of his black fur.

"Thank you, Marvin," Cam says. "I agree. No boas."

Mrow, Marvin replies.

Not giving up, Nell reaches toward a blond wig on a mannequin's head. "All right, then, how about…"

"And definitely no wigs."

Nell drops her arms to her sides, looking defeated. And annoyed. It's rare to see her lose her temper, but she's getting close with Cam. "Can you work with me a little here?"

I check the clock on the wall. "The book fair is probably being set up now. We should go soon."

Cam sighs and holds out a hand. "Let me see the cover binder again."

Nell smiles and hands over the binder. It holds color copies of dozens of different Nancy Drew covers over the years that she found online. She brought the binder to display along with my collection of Nancy Drew books.

Cam flips page after page. Finally, she stops on one. "What about this? I'll do this one."

It's a 1980s cover from the Nancy Drew Files series, where Nancy is wearing yellow shorts, a tucked-in red button-down shirt, and a white sweater draped over her shoulders with the arms loosely knotted.

"Perfect!" Nell claps her hands twice and gets to work pulling clothes from the costume racks and what she brought from home.

There's a heavy rolling sound coming from the front of the store. We turn to see my dad pushing an old grandfather clock on a dolly into our work space and across the floor toward the storage room in the back.

"Are you sure about this?" he says to my mom, who is right behind him. "It's such a cool-looking clock."

Marvin darts out and patters over to my mom, twining himself around her legs until she picks him up.

"It's a banged-up knockoff of a colonial grand-father clock," Mom says, giving Marvin head scratches. He pushes his head against her hand, his fluffy black tail hanging down and twitching from side to side. "It would cost more to fix it up than it would be worth."

"So...you're saying I can have it, then?" Dad grins at Mom. She rolls her eyes and laughs.

"That's not going in our house! It's hideous."

"It won't be hideous when I'm done with it."

"Make sure there isn't a will hidden inside," I interject.

My parents look at me curiously. I shrug. "Nancy Drew found one in an old clock once."

"Good to know," Dad says, eyeing the clock up and down like he's seeing it with new potential now.

"Oh, good grief," Mom says. "Have fun with it, whatever you do."

"You know I will!" Dad whistles as he pushes the clock through the storage room to the back door, then out into the parking lot to load into our car and drive home.

Once Cam has changed into her 1980s Nancy Drew outfit, we ride our bikes to the park. Cam has an old trailer attached to hers. She and Link used to be carted around in it as kids, apparently, but now she uses it mostly to carry books back and forth from the library. Today it holds some of our supplies—a small fold-up table, the box of Nancy Drew books, and the display posters Nell made.

In my backpack, I carry an extendable tripod for filming and my camera. Inside Nell's backpack is a clipboard with copies of the Nancy Drew quiz to hand out, and pens and pencils.

The used-book sale is set up behind Main Street in Larksville Park, on the large field of grass that sits between the community center and the fountain. I count at least twenty tables as we pedal down the footpath that runs in front of the grass. Uncle Marty the Librarian is there, and so are Calvin and a few more people from the library, all helping to set out used books and signs that mark different categories.

We decide to set up our booth at the corner of the book-sale lawn closest to the fountain. The fountain sits at a three-way intersection between the footpath and another path that leads to the lake on the opposite side of Larksville Park, so we'll have traffic from not only the book sale but also the footpath and people going in and out of the park.

We flip our kickstands down, and Cam unzips the flap of her trailer cover. I help her remove the table, and we set it up on the grass. Nell tapes her posters to the front. All three of us are stacking the Nancy Drew books on the table when a voice behind us says, "Excuse me, but what do you think you're doing?"

It's Uncle Marty the Librarian—shoulders back, crisp plaid shirt tucked in.

"Did you not see this?" He sweeps one arm to the side, indicating the rows of books behind him. "And this?" He sweeps his other arm to the side. From the shoulders down he looks like he's inviting a hug, but his face is most definitely not.

"Hi, Mr. Noys!" Nell gives him a bright smile. "Remember how we interviewed you last week for our school project? We decided to set up a booth so we could interview more people too."

"We are having a *book sale* today. This is not *Nancy Drew* Day."

He says "book sale" and "Nancy Drew" in a very exaggerated way, making big Os with his mouth, and waves a dismissive hand at our table display. I don't know if it's because I'm dressed as Nancy Drew and thereby channeling her confidence and spunk, but I'm not in the mood for his negative attitude.

"As a librarian, I'd think you'd be happy to see kids so enthusiastic about books," I say, crossing my arms. Nell and Cam step closer to me, and we all stare at Mr. Noys, waiting for a reply.

He frowns as if he doesn't understand my words. "There are so many better-written mysteries!" he insists.

"But isn't enjoying reading the point?" I say.

"Yeah," Cam says. "Would you rather have fewer people reading but everyone is reading only the books *you* think are the best—"

"And some of those people might not like the same books as you, so they might end up not wanting to read at all," Nell interjects.

"Or would you rather have everyone reading," Cam continues, "and it's a book of their choice that they are excited about?"

"And if they're excited about the book," I add, "they'll probably tell their friends, and maybe share books with each other and, I don't know—maybe even be inspired to make a documentary for a school project."

"I, well, it's just that…," Mr. Noys splutters, then brushes invisible crumbs off his sleeves. "You do make good points. But, regardless, you can't set up a 'booth' wherever you like! You need a permit for that."

"We promise not to disrupt your book sale, Mr. Noys," I say. "You won't even know we're here."

He scoffs at this and is about to say something else when Calvin walks up. "Oh, hey! Glad you could make it," he says to me and Nell and Cam, in a voice way friendlier than he ever used with us in the library.

"Hey?" I say.

"Do you need help setting up your stuff?" Then Calvin does a double take, like he's only just now noticing his uncle. "Oh! Uncle Marty. Did I forget to tell you? I hope it's okay, but I told these girls they could bring their school project today as long as they stayed out of the way of the book sale."

There's an uncomfortable silence until Uncle Marty the Librarian finally says, "Is that what happened? You told them they could do this?"

"Yeah, I figured it would be okay, since it's book-related and for school and they're not selling anything. Sorry I forgot to tell you."

"Mmm-hmm." Mr. Noys sniffs and backs away from us slowly. Then, with a pointed finger, he adds, "No trouble."

"Don't worry!" Nell reassures him.

Mr. Noys returns to the used-book fair, and Cam

says, with a bit of pride, "Who knew three sixth-grade girls armed with Nancy Drew books could be such a threat?"

Once his uncle is out of earshot, I turn to Calvin. "Thanks for your help," I say.

"Yes," Nell says. "You saved our project!"

"*Saved* is a bit dramatic," Cam says. "We would have been fine." She adjusts the sweater wrapped around her shoulders. "But thanks," she adds grudgingly.

Calvin shrugs. "No problem. I told you he doesn't like Nancy Drew."

He grins and leaves us to finish setting up our stuff.

A short while later, the book sale is bustling, and so is the footpath with people walking dogs, jogging, and pushing strollers. We've had a few people stop at our booth to look at the books and flip through Nell's cover binder. Lots of people have taken the quiz, including Calvin, who came over on a break. He got all the questions right.

Cam is recording a conversation with an older woman who stopped to admire our costumes, and

Nell is giving the Nancy Drew trivia quiz to a couple, when a familiar college-aged girl with a messenger bag draped across her back rides up on her sparkly turquoise cruiser bike.

"Hey!" Kelsey says. "It's the sisterhood of sleuths."

I can't help but smile and stand a little straighter.

"Are you selling these?" Kelsey picks up one of the books and makes a pouty face. "You should have emailed me! I might be interested."

"I'm not…They're not for sale," I reply.

"Did it turn out they're valuable? Is that why you're holding on to them?" Kelsey asks as she pages through one of the books.

"Valuable?" Between trying to figure out how the books were connected to Jacuzzi and everything with our school project, I totally forgot Maureen had mentioned they could be. "I haven't looked into that yet."

"You haven't?!" Kelsey lowers the book and looks at me in disbelief. "That's the first thing I would have done."

"The first thing I did was read them," I reply.

Kelsey laughs, like this is a hilarious joke, even though I'm telling the truth.

A bouncy movement beyond Kelsey catches my eye. I spot butterfly wings, purple cowboy boots, and a sparkly boa coming down the path. It's Gabriella, and her mom is behind her, towing Chloe and Michael in a wagon. I slink down, trying to hide behind Kelsey, and peek around her to see if Mrs. Winthrop is with them. I don't need to worry, though, because she's not.

Chloe shrieks for the wagon to stop and clambers out, followed by Michael, and then they both investigate something on the ground. After letting them stare and poke at the something, their mom ushers them back into the wagon, and the whole thing repeats itself about five steps later. Meanwhile, Gabriella keeps walking, getting farther and farther ahead of her mom and siblings.

Kelsey reaches for another of the Nancy Drew titles, and her messenger bag shifts forward, bumping the table and knocking over several books. "Oops! I'll fix it. Don't worry."

Gabriella bounds up to our booth and says, "Hi, Lava Girls! Like my boa?"

I give her a thumbs-up. Cam is still doing her interview, but Nell has just waved goodbye to the couple who took the Nancy Drew quiz. She pets the feathers Gabriella extends to her. "Very pretty!"

Gabriella looks the three of us up and down in our Nancy Drew outfits. "You like dress-up too?"

"Yes," Nell and I reply at the same time.

"No," Cam adds, having joined us after finishing the interview.

"What are you doing with that?" Gabriella points the boa at the camera on the stand.

"We're interviewing people," Nell replies.

Gabriella hops up and down. "I want to be interviewed! Interview me! My favorite color is red; my favorite animal is an elephant…"

"It's not a favorites interview," Cam says. "It's an interview about Nancy Drew. Do you know who that is?"

"Yes." Gabriella nods solemnly. She lowers her voice to a whisper and gestures for us to bend close. We do, and in a fake hushed voice, Gabriella says, "Nancy Drew is a witch who lives in a magical mushroom forest with a pet mouse named Sherman. Sherman is actually a cat who had a spell put on him."

The three of us hang there, in our forward-bent poses. Her answer is so bizarre, it makes me want to laugh, but it's also so specific and sincere, I resist the urge so I don't hurt Gabriella's feelings.

"Oooooh," Nell finally says. "That sounds like a great story."

"It is." Gabriella moves in front of our camera and strikes a pose. "You can interview me now."

Her mom reaches us then, with Chloe and Michael in the wagon. When she stops, the twins climb out. Chloe looks up at us and says, "We are looking for BUGS!" She claps her hands and does a hop-skip to where the pavement meets the grass. Michael follows, and they must have spotted something, because they both squat and stare intently at the ground.

"Gabriella, these girls are busy," their mom says.

"Oh, it's okay," Nell says.

"Yeah, it's not like we're swarmed with people who want to talk to us about Nancy Drew," Cam adds.

"That's actually why we came," Gabriella's mom says. "I'm Audrey. You gave me this flyer the other day."

She was the *only* person we handed out a flyer to, besides Annette Winthrop, so of course we remember her, but Audrey doesn't know that. I act like I'm just now remembering and say, "Oh, that's right!"

Even though nobody is standing at the camera, Gabriella is currently striking poses for it like a supermodel. Kelsey is still by our display of books, reading one of them. Without looking up, she steps to the side to make room as Audrey browses the collection. She lightly touches one of the books, then lifts it and flips through the pages. It's *The Message in the Hollow Oak*, I can't help but notice. The one Jacuzzi inscribed to Annette when they were both ten. I don't think Audrey's seen the page with the inscription, and it feels strange to know it's there and not point it out to her. But I don't, because it feels too complicated to explain how I know it's her mom.

"I wanted to ask you girls something," Audrey says, setting the book down.

"Okay." I swallow. It feels like a stone is lodged in my throat.

"How did you come by this collection?"

"I...they..." I swallow again. I wasn't expecting her to ask that, and now I'm wondering if we could get in trouble for having the books. I glance at Nell and Cam, but they look equally unsure of what to say.

Finally, I tell her the honest answer. "The books were left at my mom's store. She owns Alter Ego."

Before Audrey can respond, we're interrupted by the *shhh-shhh* of someone on skates quickly approaching us from behind. I turn and see Isabelle heading our way—when did she get Rollerblades? That's new. Her arms windmill as she struggles to balance and steer around people.

"Whhhoooaaa! Watch out!" she yells.

Splash!

ISABELLE IS HEADING STRAIGHT FOR OUR TABLE. WITHOUT MISSING a beat from her reading, Kelsey steps back toward Audrey and clears a path for Isabelle, who crashes into our booth, using it to stop herself. A wave of her strong, flowery perfume hits me and nearly knocks me over, just like the books that have fallen down again.

"Hi!" Isabelle says brightly, like she wasn't just giving me the stink eye in class the other day. It's getting exhausting not knowing whether it will be a friendly day or a snubbing day with Isabelle.

Over by the grass, Chloe bursts into tears and pushes Michael, who also starts to cry.

"I'll be right back," Audrey says.

There is a definite *We're not done here* energy to her words that nibbles away at my nerves. Audrey hurries over to the little ones. Gabriella is oblivious to her siblings' distress and has moved on from striking poses to performing a dance routine.

"What's all this?" Isabelle asks. Audrey left *The Message in the Hollow Oak* faceup on our table, and Isabelle recognizes it. "Isn't that the one from your grandmother or something? Are you selling it at the book fair?"

I glance to Audrey, who's preoccupied with her kids, and hope she didn't hear, but I'm also a little touched that Isabelle remembered. It didn't seem like she was paying attention when I showed her the book. Before I can reply, she asks another question.

"And what's with those outfits?"

That comment zaps any warm, fuzzy feelings away. I fiddle with the buttons on my blazer. It feels cartoonishly big on me all of a sudden.

"We're modeling Nancy Drew through the years," Nell says. She holds out the sides of her green dress and curtsies. "Cute, right?"

"I guess," Isabelle says.

I'm trying to think of something, anything, to say to Isabelle, but the words aren't coming. Funny how one day someone is your best friend and the next day you don't know how to talk to them anymore.

And by *funny*, I mean disappointing. Frustrating. Sad.

"Anyway," Isabelle says, "Cam, have you seen your brother? We made plans to meet in the park. He offered to help me with my Rollerblades."

Cam shakes her head. "He was shooting baskets in front of our house when I left this morning. I thought he was going to Ben's house later."

Isabelle's eyes widen in a way I recognize. I've seen this face several times before, but a specific occasion comes to mind. It was earlier this year, on her eleventh birthday. I was invited to go with her and her parents to a fondue restaurant to celebrate. We were at her house that afternoon, decorating cupcakes, when the phone rang. Izzy's mom walked into another room with the phone, but we could still hear her side of the conversation loud and clear.

She said: "What do you mean the meeting went late? You're going to miss your flight!"

And: "There absolutely *was* something you could have done. You could have said, 'It's my daughter's birthday. I have to go.' Simple as that. I can't believe you would do this."

And: "No, we can't just go another night. Her birthday is today. We have plans for *this* night."

During that moment, Izzy had that wide-eyed, trying-not-to-cry look on her face. Eventually she said, "Siri, play show tunes," and upped the volume on "Waving Through a Window" until it drowned out her mom's voice. She concentrated on placing flower-shaped sprinkles on her cupcake, and so I did the same. We went to the fondue restaurant with her mom, who said a girls' night out would be better anyway. And it was fun and we laughed, so maybe she was right, but all night I replayed Izzy's mom saying *I can't believe you would do this* in my head and wondered if Izzy was doing the same.

At our Nancy Drew booth, Isabelle blinks, and the hurt expression is replaced with a bored *whatever* face. She drags a finger lightly across the tops of the Nancy Drew books, like she's daring herself to touch them, and it reminds me of her fear of old things.

A couple of weeks ago, I might have teased her about that. I can imagine it as clearly as if the old Maizy and Izzy were here in the park. Me breathing in the smell of a book, then offering it to a cringing Izzy, who runs away, giggling. I chase her, saying, "Smell the book! Just one whiff!"

But I don't tease her today. I don't say anything. Isabelle lifts her finger, and with a slight shudder she says, "Well, have fun with this."

She starts to wobble away on her skates, but before she gets too far, words I didn't know I was going to say bubble out of my mouth.

"Do you want to help us?" I ask her back. "You can if you want."

Isabelle swivels around. I'm anticipating a smile, or at least more of her bored expression, but instead she looks like I've pushed her.

"Oh, can I?" she says sarcastically.

Her words are a slap, and I immediately feel stupid for saying anything. Stupid for worrying about Izzy's feelings when this *Isabelle* person doesn't seem to care about mine.

The sarcasm continues. "Doing someone else's school project sounds super fun, but no thanks."

Gabriella is still dancing her routine, and she swings her boa to the ground just in time for Isabelle to roll over it when she turns to skate away. Only with Isabelle's unsteady step-slide skating and Gabriella's wiggling of the boa, it somehow gets wrapped up in the wheels.

Everything happens so quickly, it's like a fast-forward button was pressed. One minute, Gabriella is smiling and animated and Isabelle is snarky and upset. The next, Gabriella is tugging her boa with frustration, not realizing it's stuck, and Isabelle is panicked, not realizing why her wheel stopped turning. She does a few hop-hop steps and shrieks, her arms waving more wildly than before. She rolls straight to the fountain and bends forward, probably hoping to use the side to stop her like she did with our table, but instead, she slides over the top and rolls into the water, landing with a giant splash.

For a split second, I think of crashing my bike in the lobster costume and how Isabelle did nothing. And how once I'd helped myself out of that embarrassing situation, she made it worse.

Isabelle sits up, gasping and wailing in the water. If I wanted to, I could do the same thing. This could be my payback moment. The fountain is far enough away from our table, I could busy myself rearranging the books and pretend not to have seen. Or I could walk away in the opposite direction down the footpath and ask people if they want to take our quiz.

But I don't do any of that. Izzy sits up, and I run forward and grab her hand. She's so upset, I'm not sure she registers that it's me helping her. I try to pull her up, but the bottom of the fountain must be slippery, plus she has the Rollerblades on, plus she's not trying to help herself. Nell grabs her other hand, and Cam pulls off her own socks and shoes and jumps into the water to stand behind Izzy, lifting her from the armpits.

The shock of what happened wears off slightly, and Izzy starts to cooperate, and together the four of us get her up and out of the fountain. She's dripping wet, so I unbutton my blazer and offer it to her, but she pushes it away.

"I don't want your stupid jacket, Maizy. Just leave me alone."

Isabelle wobble-step-skates back the way she came, a trail of water dripping behind her.

"Wow," Nell says quietly.

Gabriella and her siblings are hopping around us now. They ran over to the fountain because of the commotion. Chloe tries to climb in, probably because she saw Izzy and Cam in the water, but Audrey hurries over and pulls her back by the shirt.

"Are you three okay?" Audrey asks us.

We nod, and she focuses on me. "I want to make sure I tell you this before my kids cause more ruckus—I left those books at your mom's store." She tucks her hair behind an ear.

"*You* did?" I repeat. "Why?"

Behind Audrey, Cam's mouth drops open and Nell covers hers. They go sit beside the kids on the fountain wall, signaling they'll keep an eye on them while we talk.

"I don't really know your mom," Audrey says. "At least as a grown-up I don't. She actually used to babysit me. But I knew she was your grandmother's daughter, and I knew she owned Alter Ego. And my mother and your grandmother were once the best of friends."

I don't want to sound rude and say, *I know this already*, so I simply nod.

"My father recently passed, and for some reason this prompted my mother to purge a lot of her things. She calls it Swedish death cleaning. She can't bring herself to touch Dad's stuff yet, and so she's redirecting her energy toward her own.

"Anyway. I've been helping her, and one day, I saw she'd put that box of books in the donation pile. I looked through them, thinking maybe Gabriella would want to read them one day, and all these memories came back. Oh, my mom loved Nancy Drew! She read the books to me when I was little—she even had a board game that we played, although I don't know what happened to that. And I remembered her best friend—your grandmother. I was often brought along with them to garage sales as they searched for more books to add to their collections. And when your mom used to babysit me, I remember asking her to read me a Nancy Drew book, and she'd pretend to hate them. She'd wave her hands and say, 'No, no, not another one!' I thought this was the funniest thing, so of course I only wanted her to read even more."

"That does sound like my mom. I don't think she was pretending, though."

Audrey is surprised to hear this. "Oh, I didn't realize…"

I don't want her to feel bad for bringing any of this up, so I add, "But I could be wrong."

Audrey nods. "The thing is, I'm not sure why my mom and your grandmother stopped spending time together, but my mom could use a friend these days. And a friendship like theirs isn't easy to come by. But I knew she wouldn't want to reach out. And I didn't want to…" Audrey pauses, trying to think of the right word.

"Meddle?" I suggest.

"Yes! She'd be upset if I meddled, but I also couldn't just sit by and do nothing. So I tried to give fate a nudge in the right direction. I did a little sleuthing of my own and learned your mom owns Alter Ego, and then one morning before I could talk myself out of it, I left the box outside. I tucked a photo of my mom and your grandmother on top, hoping your mom would see it and recognize it and everything would unfold naturally from there."

"Things definitely unfolded from there," I agree. I don't want to get into explaining all that happened, but I do tell her that I found the photo and figured out the connection between Jacuzzi and Annette Winthrop.

"I also wanted to reunite them," I tell Audrey. "I was going to try to bring them together, but it didn't work."

I explain how the box of books inspired our Nancy Drew documentary and everything we'd been working on.

"You know," she says, "I think bringing them together is a great idea, and maybe your documentary is the answer to how we do that."

Audrey shares her idea with me, and I think it's perfect. Then she gathers her kids, and they wave and head home. Cam, Nell, and I walk back to our table, but I stop short in front of it.

My camera is still on its stand. Our bikes are on the grass. The posters are taped to the front of the table, and the books are still on top.

Most of the books.

The Message in the Hollow Oak, the one with the inscription from Jacuzzi, is nowhere to be seen.

20

Thief!

"IT WAS RIGHT HERE," I SAY. I TAP THE TABLE. "RIGHT HERE."

Audrey had flipped through it and then set it down. Did anyone else come by and look at it?

We scan the area around us, as if we're going to see the thief holding the book and waving to us. People travel along the footpath as usual, and more people browse the used-book sale. A cyclist cruises past the fountain. Everything is typical Saturday-morning-at-the-park, and nobody looks suspicious.

I retrace my steps to the fountain, trying to remember everything that happened. Izzy fell in, we ran over, Audrey and the kids came over, and Izzy stormed off. Audrey and I had that conversation while Nell and Cam kept an eye on the kids.

Who could have taken that book?

I walk back to our table, observing everything around us. Maybe someone browsing the book sale thought our books were part of it? But Calvin is at the checkout table, helping ring people up. He would have recognized the Nancy Drew book as ours if someone tried to buy it.

Mr. Noys wasn't happy about us setting up this table, and he's not a fan of Nancy Drew, but he wouldn't have taken one of the books to spite us, would he? I scan the book fair until I spot him, stooping to pick up a book that fell on the grass. He sets it back on a table. He's not acting like someone who just stole a book, but then no decent thief would want to give themselves away, right?

In the Nancy Drew books, footprints are often helpful clues, so I scan the ground around the table. No footprints. No dropped pieces of litter or any telling objects that I can find. Then I notice an area where the grass is a little mashed. I get closer to investigate. The grass is pressed down in a long, narrow line that starts near our table, crosses the corner of grass, and exits onto the path deeper in the park. It looks like someone either dragged something small and heavy or—

"It's a bike trail," Cam says, observing the pressed-down grass with me.

And just like that, I remember a certain turquoise cruiser and a messenger bag that can hold an incredible number of books.

"It was Kelsey," I say. "She stole the book!"

"Are you sure?" Cam asks.

"Kelsey wouldn't do that," Nell insists. "She helped us with our project."

"She was the last person I saw looking at the books. And from the very beginning when I met her, she's been interested in how valuable those books might be. Maybe she figured out that edition was worth something."

I jump on my bike, ready to go after her, but Cam raises a hand. "Hold on, we need a plan. We should split up to have a better chance of finding her."

"Someone should stay at the table too," Nell says. "To keep an eye on the rest of our stuff. And maybe it was an accident and she'll bring it back soon."

"I have the trailer on my bike, so you both will be able to ride faster," Cam says. "I'll stay here."

"I'll ride to the community center," Nell volunteers.

"And I'll check the opposite side of the park."

Nell and I jump on our bikes, pedal into the park, and split off in different directions when the path breaks in two. I pass the playground and the Lark and round one side of the lake, scouting for Kelsey as I go, but I don't see her anywhere. There's a fork in the path up ahead. One way will take me out of the park and into the wealthy neighborhood. The other meanders toward the Larksville College campus.

The college! Of course. The campus *has* to be where Kelsey's headed. I can't believe I didn't think of that right away.

I pedal as fast as I can, aware that Kelsey has a head start. She doesn't know anyone is pursuing her, though, so hopefully I can find her.

I crest a hill, and below there's a bicyclist on a sparkling blue bike with a messenger bag on her back. She's riding at a normal pace, and with the slope giving me an extra dose of speed, I'm soon within calling distance.

"Kelsey!" I shout. "Wait!"

The words come out before I realize it's probably a dumb idea to signal to a thief that you're behind them. But it would make a funny scene in one of my movies…

> **MAIZY:** Excuse me, robber, I see you've stolen my wallet.
> **THIEF:** Why, yes, I did! Would you like it back now?
> **MAIZY:** Yes, please.
> **THIEF:** Here you go. Sorry for any trouble!
> **MAIZY:** No problem. Have a great day!

Maybe my imagined scenario isn't as ridiculous as I thought, because Kelsey hears me call her name and stops. I slow down as I approach her, panting from pedaling so fast.

Kelsey smiles and says, "Hey! Did you want to interview me for your thing?"

She's trying to distract and disarm me, isn't she? I'm not falling for her ploys.

I straddle my bike and speak as firmly as I can so she knows I mean business. "I know you stole my book. You need to give it back, right now."

That knocks the smile off her face.

"You think I did what?" Kelsey asks.

"You know what you did," I say.

Now she's definitely not smiling, and in fact she looks very annoyed with me. Angry even.

"No, I don't know. You think I stole something?"

My face is flushed already, but it heats up even more. She's trying to trick me...right?

"You were the last one by our Nancy Drew books," I insist. "And you've had your eye on them since we met. And now one's gone."

"There's a book missing?!"

Kelsey's incredulous tone is very convincing. Either she's a great actor or...

"Yes," I say, the forcefulness dropped from my voice.

"So, you thought I'd *steal* yours? Just because I admired them and happened to be nearby?"

I know I should drop this. I've obviously offended her, but also, wouldn't it make sense for a thief to act offended for exactly that reason? So that I'd feel bad for accusing her and leave her alone? There's one way to know for sure.

"Look, I realize I've probably made a mistake. But could you show me the inside of your bag? If you really didn't steal anything, then you have nothing to hide."

Kelsey frowns and yanks open her messenger bag to show me. My heart sinks. There's a wallet, keys, a phone, fingerless gloves, lip balm…All sorts of things, but no book.

"I'm so sorry," I mumble. "I just don't know what could have happened to it."

Kelsey sighs. "It's okay. If I was the only person you saw near them, I guess it makes sense you might suspect me."

"I'm really sorry," I say again. And I mean it. Not just for accusing her of stealing the book, but for everything. For thinking she could have stolen an eraser from Turn the Page, for not trusting that her offers to help were genuine.

"Just…when you're solving your mysteries, be careful who you go around accusing, okay?"

I ride slowly back to our table, still feeling bad for accusing Kelsey and confused about what must have happened. I think through the events again. If Kelsey didn't take that book, how did it disappear?

When I turn down the path leading back to our booth, I see Nell has returned and is standing with Cam. Marching across the grass toward them is Mr. Noys. He does not look happy. And there's a book in his hand.

21

Caught Wet-Handed

I REACH THE BOOTH JUST AS UNCLE MARTY THE LIBRARIAN DROPS *The Message in the Hollow Oak* on the table. It's damp and dirty, and a soggy napkin is stuck to one side, and another has some kind of smear that I hope is chocolate.

"What happened?!" I ask.

"That's what I would like to know," he says. "I may not want to use precious space in the library for an old series like this, but that doesn't mean it should be trashed. This book was in perfectly good condition. Some collector out there would have been thrilled to have it."

"It was…trashed?" I ask.

Cam brings the book closer to her nose and sniffs, then flinches. "This smells."

"I did just say it was in the trash," Mr. Noys says.

"Did someone throw out a bunch of roses too? Because whew."

Cam holds the book toward me to smell, and I start to rear back. But then I recognize the scent and grab the book from her, smelling again to be sure.

I look at the ruined book and sigh.

"Izzy," I say.

I'm back on my bike, pedaling across the park again, but this time I'm heading to our spot, the hidden clearing among the evergreens. I don't know why I'm convinced that's where she went—maybe because I know Izzy goes there when she's upset, or maybe it's wishful thinking.

I have no idea what I'll say if I find her. I don't even know how I'm feeling. My emotions churn as

I pedal: confused, hurt, angry, sad. Confused, hurt, angry, sad. Round and round they go. I think of all the times recently that she's snapped at me, the up-and-down way she's been treating me, and now she's ruined a book that she knew was important to me. Why? What have I done to her? By the time I reach the evergreens, the only feeling going around is angry, angry, angry, angry.

I drop my bike and slide between two bushy, bristly pines. Needles rain on my helmet and cling to my shirt as I step into the clearing. Izzy sits hunched on the boulder, her back to me, sobbing into her knees. The Rollerblades are off and discarded on the ground. She doesn't look up until I'm standing right next to her. Mascara streaks run down her cheeks. (When did she start wearing makeup?)

I don't like seeing her cry, but also, shouldn't I be the one who's upset?

"You knew the book was important to me. Why would you destroy it?"

I expect to hear an angry Isabelle retort, or maybe to be ignored. But she launches up, and I flinch, not sure what's going to happen. She throws her arms around me and cries into my shoulder.

"I'm sorry," she says.

My anger dwindles, like she's squeezing it out with her hug. I don't know if she's apologizing for stealing the book, for snubbing me, for not doing the Shellfish Holmes project the way we planned, for all of the above, or for something else entirely.

We sit together on the boulder. Isabelle sniffles and wipes her face with a corner of her shirt.

I take a deep breath and say, "I just don't understand...Why did you do that to my book?"

"I don't know. I was mad and took it without really thinking. It was a stupid thing to do. I just wish..." She tugs at a loose string on her shorts. "I wish things were different."

"Different how?"

She doesn't answer at first and continues to fiddle with her shorts.

"Lots of ways," she finally says.

Then, speaking more to her lap than to me, she adds, "You always want to do the same stuff we've

done since third grade. Making movies and playing with stuffies…"

I almost want to point out I'm not using stuffies for the documentary, but I stop myself. What's wrong with using stuffies for a movie if I want to?

"I *like* doing those things," I say. "And it's fun doing them with you."

"Yeah, we did have fun. But…don't you want to try something different? We could do each other's makeup or paint our nails. Maybe try out for volleyball together?"

Nothing she lists sounds fun to me at all.

"I've been pretty happy doing everything we usually do," I say.

"Well, I guess I haven't." She looks sad about it, as if she was hoping I'd say, *Yes! Forget the movie stuff! I want to do all that instead!*

After a beat she adds, "I'm really sorry about the book. I'll pay you back for it. Or buy you a new one."

"It's not about the money," I say. "It hurts that you'd ruin something I care about."

Isabelle sniffs, the tears starting up again. "I know," she whispers. "I'm really sorry."

"It's okay," I say. Not because I'm okay with what she did. What's done is done, and she can't take back her actions, but I believe her when she says she's sorry for what she did. I swing an arm around her shoulders and give Izzy—Isabelle—another hug. It feels like goodbye, and maybe in some ways it is.

We sit quietly for a minute. The sun shines down on us, but the air is crisp and cool, filled with the sweet woodsy smell of the trees and dusty dirt. I'm thinking about how our friendship has been like walking in the park. And maybe I've been trying to keep us on the same path we've always walked together, but Isabelle wants to try a new way. Maybe there's room for me on that path, but I'm happy where I'm at. I don't want to change my direction right now. We can be on different paths and still be friends. Maybe not the same kind of friends as before. But it doesn't have to be all or nothing. And maybe our paths will reconnect in the future, like they did for me and Nell. Like I'm hoping they will for Jacuzzi and Annette.

"So you're trying new things, like Rollerblading?" I finally say, nudging the discarded skates with my shoe. It's a risk, a teasing joke, so I smile to show I mean it in a friendly way. Isabelle rolls her eyes but returns the smile.

"Yes, actually. Like Rollerblading." She reaches down to put one of the skates back on. "I'm going to master these dumb skates, whether Link helps me or not."

I hand her the other skate.

"You will. You can do anything you put your mind to, Isabelle."

22

The Screening

FOR THE REST OF THE WEEKEND, NELL, CAM, AND I EDIT THE DOCU-
mentary. I have to say, I'm pretty proud of our work.
I'm also a little sad that it's all coming to an end. Sunday afternoon, the three of us are sprawled around
my bedroom. I'm sitting in my desk chair, swiveling
back and forth. Cam is lying across my bed on her
back, trying to solve my Rubik's Cube. Nell is flipping through one of the Nancy Drew books.

"It's going to be weird, not having this project to
work on," I say.

"It was so much more fun than doing a fashion show by myself would have been," Nell says.

"And it was a billion times better than working on *Sherlock Nose*," Cam adds.

"We should sit together at lunch this week..." The words come out of my mouth, and then I immediately wish I could put them back in. Nell and Cam probably have other people they'd rather sit with— Cam's probably with friends from the soccer team, and I think Nell bounces around different activities and groups. The silent origami club lunches aren't *so* bad.

"We totally should," Nell says.

"How about tomorrow?" Cam asks. "We'll need to celebrate when our documentary is chosen for the Curio."

We all laugh and cheer at that. It makes me feel hopeful that maybe some things aren't coming to an end.

Mr. Orson lets us have popcorn in class Monday morning as we watch the different projects. One group chose live musical for their storytelling method and history for their genre, performing songs they wrote about Eleanor Roosevelt. You can tell they were inspired by *Hamilton*, and their singing is really good. Another group does modern dance for their storytelling method and science fiction for genre. That one is a bit out there—I think it's about a battle between aliens, but since there are no words, I'm not sure if I'm interpreting it right. There are several fairy-tale retellings, both in movie format and live plays.

And *Sherlock Nose* isn't horrible—it gets the most laughs for sure. When the culprit in the mystery is revealed to be an evil twin, Cam loudly whispers to Nell and me, "Told you it would make a good twist!"

And then it's our turn to share our documentary, *On the Case of Nancy Drew*. The opening shot is Main Street, early in the morning, when it's super quiet. My voice narrates: "One day, I was helping my mom at her shop when I heard this thud out front."

It cuts to my feet walking through the store, the door opening with the jingle of the bell. Even Marvin participated in the reenactment, just like he did the day the books showed up.

My voice continues the story: "Someone had left a cardboard box. I didn't think much of it at first—it's an antiques and thrift store, so it's not unusual for people to drop off stuff they don't want. But when I looked inside the box, it was filled with dozens of original editions of Nancy Drew books. Even stranger than that, there was an old photo of my grandmother inside too.

"My grandmother didn't know anything about the books or the photo or why the box had shown up. But like Nancy Drew with a hunch, I couldn't shake the feeling that there must be more to the story. So I did what any good sleuth would do: gathered some friends and looked for clues." As I say that line in the movie, there's a shot of me, Nell, and Cam riding our bikes together at sunset.

At the end of our documentary, we get a nice round of applause. I really do think we're a front-runner for the Curio. Mr. Orson collects votes at the end of class and silently counts the results.

"All right, the project that will be representing our class at the Curio is…"

We all drum the tops of our desks, and Mr. Orson shouts, "*Eleanor!*"

The whole class hesitates after he makes the announcement, probably because most everyone was hoping to be chosen themselves. And then we all clap and congratulate the winners.

"They were really good," Nell says.

"They deserved it," Cam says.

I voted for *Eleanor*, so I can't disagree. I thought I would be more disappointed that I wasn't going to have a project shown at the Curio after all, but surprisingly, I feel okay. Maybe that's because I know I have plenty more movies in me. I know I'll have one screened at the Curio someday.

Or maybe it's because I already have plans in the works for a different screening of our documentary. It won't be at the Curio, but I hope it will be just as meaningful.

At lunch, Nell, Cam, and I eat on the grass on the west side of school.

"What are we going to work on next?" Cam asks.

"Next?" I repeat.

"Yeah, maybe we could submit something for the Curio's Winter Festival."

"Yes! Something with good costume potential," Nell says, and almost immediately snaps her fingers. "I've got it! Your mom has those amazing flapper dresses at her store—we could do something set in the 1920s."

Cam groans. "I'm not wearing one of those dresses."

The 1920s make me think of a black-and-white noir-style detective movie. Perhaps my *Shellfish Holmes* script could have its day after all.

"How would you feel about being a lobster?" I ask Cam.

⸺

Friday evening, I'm hosting a screening of the Nancy Drew documentary in my backyard. There's a screen and projector set up, with chairs and cushions gathered in front for seating. A tablet is propped on one chair for Max. We'll connect with him right before we start so he can watch too. As the guests arrive,

Nell hands out the programs we made, and Cam hands out cups of popcorn.

Jacuzzi's walking boot is still on, so Dad drove her over, and she's the first to arrive. She's dressed thematically for Nancy Drew with a cloche hat, a 1930s-style dress, and a magnifying glass dangling around her neck. Soon, our backyard is filled with Cam's and Nell's families, Professor Vale, Kelsey, Maureen, Uncle Marty the Librarian, and Calvin.

"Is that everyone?" Dad asks. He's eager to make an announcement.

"Almost," I say.

I wait out front, and finally a minivan pulls up. The back door slides open, and Gabriella hops out and runs up to our door.

"I am ready for the movies!" she announces.

I direct her to the backyard, and she's off.

Chloe climbs out of the van as Audrey unbuckles Michael. The front passenger door opens, and out steps Mrs. Winthrop. She looks uncertainly at our house and then says something to Audrey.

I hear Audrey reply, "It's okay, Mom."

Before they get to the front door, I run to find Jacuzzi. Most everyone is in the backyard, but Jacuzzi is in the kitchen.

"I have a surprise for you," I say.

"For me?" She smiles. "This is your night, Maizy."

"Well, this has to do with Nancy Drew. And…I don't know if you'll like it, but I hope you do. Will you come with me?"

Jacuzzi walks with me out the front door and stops short. Audrey and her mom are there, halfway up our walk.

"Oh," Jacuzzi says. "Annette."

"Hi, Susie," Annette says.

"Let's go to the party!" Chloe bellows, and charges up the path, Michael running behind.

Audrey and I exchange looks. I think we're both unsure about leaving Jacuzzi and Annette, but also someone should be minding the little ones. Fortunately, Nell appears in the doorway. She greets Chloe and Michael and ushers them inside, giving us a thumbs-up and then closing the door.

I'm about to explain, or maybe apologize, to Jacuzzi and Annette. I wrote down some notes last night of what I might say: that I appreciate their being here and that Audrey and I were afraid neither would come if she knew the other was going to be there, so we kept it a secret, and they don't have to do anything but watch the documentary, but I thought they might like reconnecting because I know they were important friends to each other at one time...

I'm still mentally preparing myself to say something, when Jacuzzi says, "I'm so sorry about George, Annette."

Mrs. Winthrop nods, blinking away tears. "Thank you. And I'm sorry about...everything."

"Oh, well." Jacuzzi waves a hand like *No big deal.*

"No, really. I am. I wasn't there for you when you needed a friend. And I regret that. I don't know what I was thinking. It's not like divorce is contagious."

Jacuzzi hoots her surprised little laugh, then quiets. "Yes, well, I appreciate that. I really do. But it rattles us when things change that we don't see coming. I understand that."

Yes, I think. *I understand that too.*

"Come on." Jacuzzi steps to the side, making room for Annette. "Let's go watch this documentary I've heard rave reviews about."

Jacuzzi and Annette link arms and walk up the path and into the house.

Audrey and I watch them go, and she lifts a hand to her face and swipes away a tear. "Thank you for doing this, Maizy. I think it's going to be a good thing."

Everyone finds a seat, and we connect with Max, so he's there on the tablet. Dad steps in front of the movie screen, clinking a spoon against a glass for quiet. "I'll keep this short so we can get to the main event. But I wanted to present something to Maizy. This is a 'just because' gift—just because I had the idea for it."

I realize now there's something nearly as tall and wide as my dad in front of his shed, and it's covered with a sheet. He walks over to stand next to it and says, "I didn't find a will inside, but all the same I hope you like it."

He yanks the sheet and reveals the beat-up grandfather clock he took out of Alter Ego, only he's fixed it up and painted it blue. But that's not the coolest part. Through the glass door, I can see that the inside has been customized with bookshelves that hold my collection of Nancy Drews.

I give him a big hug. "I love it!" I say, and take a minute to open and close the door and slide a book out.

"I'm still working on a name," Dad says. "I was thinking Grandpa Shelfie."

There's laughter from everyone gathered in our yard. Gabriella stands on her chair and raises a hand. Audrey whispers at her to sit down, but Dad says, "It's okay—do you have a question?"

"I think you should call it the Book Eater, because there's books in its belly." She dissolves in giggles.

Mr. Noys speaks up. "Or how about Ticktock Treasures?"

"Drew O'Clock?" Cam suggests.

"The Crime Chime!" Maureen volunteers.

I hug Dad again, and everyone settles in to watch the documentary. Nell, Cam, and I introduce our project. We keep it simple, thank everyone for coming, and press play.

The backyard fills with our voices narrating what we learned about Nancy Drew, Carolyn Keene, Mildred Wirt Benson, and the generations of readers who have been fans, interspersed with clips of our different interviews.

I stand to one side of the screen and take in these faces, glowing in the light of something I've created. Really, it kind of astounds me to think about all of us gathered here. I didn't know most of these people very well, or even at all, only weeks ago. And now there are threads between us, threads that travel back in time nearly one hundred years to a man who had the idea for a teenage female sleuth and the woman who typed the words that breathed life into Nancy Drew.

When the documentary ends, everyone applauds. There are hugs and congratulations and a general feeling of festivity. Calvin is talking to Professor Vale while Nell's parents chat with Cam and Link's mom. Kelsey, Cam, and Nell play a round of Simon Says with the younger kids while Nell's little brother and Link kick a soccer ball back and forth on the grass. Dad is showing Mr. Noys and Maureen the clock bookcase.

As I walk by, I hear Maureen say, "Something like this would be fun to display in the bookstore."

"The library too," Mr. Noys adds. "Perhaps we could commission your work?"

"I'd love that," Dad says. "I'll look into sourcing more old clocks, or I bet I could salvage other interesting pieces. Maybe an abandoned refrigerator or..."

His voice blends into the chatter of the backyard as I approach Jacuzzi and Annette, who are standing with Mom and Audrey.

"So," I ask Jacuzzi, "did you like it?"

"Like it?" Jacuzzi hugs me. "I loved it! You never cease to amaze me, Maizy."

"Maizy," Annette says, and I straighten, a little nervous about what she might say. "I'm so glad those old books found their way to you. It makes me happy to know they're with a true Nancy Drew fan, and I thank you for bringing these two old chums together again." She bumps her hip against Jacuzzi's.

"Do you remember that Nancy Drew game we used to play?" Jacuzzi asks. "How did it go?"

Mom groans and smiles. "Oh, I remember this! You made me play it on road trips. It worked like this: First, we need three random skills. You pick one, Audrey—anything that pops into your head."

"Singing," Audrey replies.

Mom points to Jacuzzi, who offers "knitting," then Annette, who suggests "speaking French."

"Okay, now we devise a mystery that involves Nancy using all three skills in order to solve it."

"Maizy, you're a wonderful storyteller," Annette says. "Why don't you get us started?"

The wheels are already turning, so I'm ready. "Nancy is in a choir—no, she's Christmas caroling with Bess and George."

"A holiday-themed mystery!" Jacuzzi says. "I love those."

"A woman comes running out of her house, super upset," I continue.

"But she's speaking French!" Mom interjects.

"Yes! She's super upset in French, but fortunately Nancy has been taking a night class to learn the language. She's able to understand that the woman has just been robbed. The girls see footsteps in the snow from the thief, so they follow them."

The knitting talent stumps me into silence, but Audrey chimes in. "Nancy knit Bess and George long scarves for Christmas, and she knit one for herself too—"

"Blue, of course," Annette says, "because Nancy loves all things blue."

Everyone laughs, and I continue. "They spot the thief hiding the stolen goods in a shed. He hasn't heard or seen Nancy and her friends yet—"

"Because of the snow," Mom says.

"And so the girls tie their scarves together and use them to first trip the thief, then tie him up while they wait for the police to arrive," I finish.

"Brilliant!" Jacuzzi says. She begins clapping, and the others join in.

"That was actually fun," Mom says. "Maybe I should have given those books a chance when I was younger."

"You still can!" Annette says.

"You can borrow mine if you want," I add.

"Maybe I will," Mom says, throwing an arm around my shoulders. "It's never too late to try something new, is it?"

"Or revisit something old," Jacuzzi adds.

I scan the backyard again, wanting to remember this evening. A few weeks ago, I never would have predicted this night. Everything was so different then. I was happy with how things were and didn't want anything to change.

But the thing about change is, you can't stop it. Even if you stand still and do absolutely nothing, the seasons change around you. If it's going to happen, you might as well keep walking and enjoy the path ahead.

❧·AUTHOR'S NOTE·❧

This book is a work of fiction, but Maizy's story was inspired by both the history of Nancy Drew and my lifelong fascination with the young sleuth.

I first met Nancy Drew on a summer trip to my aunt and uncle's house in San Diego when I was seven. This was the mid-eighties, in the time before portable gaming devices, tablets, e-readers, YouTube, and streaming shows available at any hour. I had finished the books I'd brought on the drive down. The adults and teenagers were interested in talking and listening to records, not the Uno and Monopoly marathons I was angling for. I had no similar-aged friend to play imagination games with in the backyard.

In short: I was bored.

Sensing this, my aunt offered me a cardboard box filled with sixteen assorted titles from the original Nancy Drew Mystery Stories. Once I started reading, I was hooked. I sprawled in front of a fan, and Nancy Drew and her chums took center stage while the conversations and music of my family faded in the background.

What I admired about Nancy Drew were her friendships, her smarts, and her ability to problem-solve just about any situation. Everyone respected and listened to her. And the stories were exciting—unexpected twists and turns and peril that ended nearly every chapter with a cliffhanger. But Nancy always kept her cool. Scenarios that would have frightened me didn't frighten Nancy. Batman and Spider-Man are childhood superhero idols for some; mine was Nancy Drew.

My aunt let me bring the books home, and once I'd read them all, I went to the library to seek out more. There I discovered the digest-size paperbacks—a continuation of the original series in a different format produced by another publisher—and the Nancy Drew Files, a modernized take on the teen sleuth. Nancy Drew sparked my love for the mystery genre and for a well-paced story, and soon I was branching out to try a variety of authors and series.

When I was in my early twenties, I learned that Carolyn Keene, the author of the Nancy Drew series, wasn't a real person. While I'd known some people wrote under pseudonyms, I had no idea that authors could be entirely made up, fictional characters themselves. I love learning the stories behind a story, so I sought out more information about Carolyn Keene and how Nancy Drew came to be, and soon I realized the history of Nancy Drew might be even more fascinating than the mysteries themselves.

Nancy Drew was the brainchild of Edward Stratemeyer, who began the Stratemeyer Syndicate in 1905. He had the notion to hire writers to pen his many ideas for different children's series, with each series assigned a fictional author, like Carolyn Keene. The writers were paid a flat fee to turn around a draft of the contracted book in a set amount of time, typically about a month. The rights to the story, as well as the series' pseudonym, belonged to the Stratemeyer Syndicate, which meant the writers did not earn royalties and agreed not to use the pseudonym with any of their own writing outside the contracted work. Edward provided the writer with character notes and an outline. He edited the books and sold them to various publishers. By the time Nancy Drew came on the scene in 1930, Edward Stratemeyer was managing more than thirty different series, each with books published every year.

Prior to Nancy Drew, Edward had already published a number of successful series with strong female leads, such as the Moving Picture Girls series by Laura Lee Hope, the Outdoor Girls series by Laura Lee Hope, and the Ruth Fielding series by Alice B. Emerson.

In 1926, he noted the popularity of detective novels and decided to try a similar series for young readers. The result was the Hardy Boys, which was a success, and in 1929 Edward pitched a series to Grosset & Dunlap similar to the Hardy Boys but with a female teenage sleuth, who he suggested could be named Stella Strong. The publisher agreed to the project but opted to call her Nancy Drew.

Edward had a ghostwriter in mind for the Nancy Drew series: Mildred Wirt Benson, who was writing the final books in his Ruth Fielding series. He asked her to write "a breeder set"—the first three titles to be published simultaneously to launch this new series. Mildred agreed and was paid $125 per book.

Many have described Mildred Wirt Benson as the embodiment of Nancy Drew. She was an ambitious, determined woman who faced challenges head-on. In 1927, she was the first person to receive a master's degree in journalism from the University of Iowa. She was an athlete and championship diver. She published 135 children's novels and worked as a journalist for fifty-eight years, right up to the day she died, at age ninety-six. Mildred loved to travel and had long been interested in aviation. She earned her commercial pilot's license when she was fifty-nine.

On April 28, 1930, *The Secret of the Old Clock*, *The Hidden Staircase*, and *The Bungalow Mystery* were published. Two weeks later, Edward Stratemeyer contracted pneumonia and died at the age of sixty-seven. When he died, he took with him much of the knowledge of the inner workings of his business, and the future of the Stratemeyer Syndicate was uncertain. His daughters, Harriet Stratemeyer Adams and Edna Stratemeyer Squier, took over. Edna ultimately became more of a silent partner, but Harriet was hands-on and committed to continuing the legacy of her father's work.

Mildred Wirt Benson was already working on the fourth Nancy Drew when Edward Stratemeyer passed away. Harriet continued to hire her, and ultimately Mildred wrote twenty-three of the first thirty titles in the Nancy Drew Mystery Stories collection. These titles were published from 1930 to 1953.

Although Mildred Wirt Benson is best known for being the first Carolyn Keene, she spent much of her life without acknowledgment for her role in launching a series that would transcend "phenomenon" as Nancy Drew and her stories continue to be passed from one generation to the next. Mildred even had the experience of someone else taking credit for her work and being celebrated for it. That someone was Harriet Stratemeyer Adams. While Harriet did take over writing the Nancy Drew Mystery Stories from number thirty-one on, she also began to say in interviews that she was and always had been Carolyn Keene. In *Girl Sleuth: Nancy Drew and the Women Who Created Her*, Melanie Rehak recounts, "Harriet's standard story was that Edward had died leaving behind only drafts of the first three Nancy Drews, and that she had taken on the series—as well as the whole company—single-handedly from there, rewriting those rudimentary manuscripts."[1]

In 1980, the year Nancy Drew turned fifty, Harriet Adams and the Stratemeyer Syndicate became involved in a lawsuit involving Grosset & Dunlap, the original publisher for the series, and Simon & Schuster, the new publisher. Mildred Wirt Benson was one of the witnesses for Grosset & Dunlap. As part of her testimony, she shared evidence of her role in creating Nancy Drew and the books she wrote, thereby putting it on public record that she was the original Carolyn Keene. There is an often-told story about Harriet Stratemeyer and Mildred Wirt Benson meeting on that day in court, which Rehak describes: "Upon seeing Mildred, whom she was not expecting and did not recognize without an introduction, Harriet uttered a single, amazed sentence: 'I thought you were dead.'"[2]

Even though Mildred Wirt Benson testified to being Carolyn Keene, little fanfare or attention was made of that moment outside the courtroom. In fact, it wasn't until the University of Iowa decided to host a Nancy Drew Conference thirteen years later, in 1993, and invited Mildred Wirt Benson as an honored guest that she garnered any acclaim. Mildred was eighty-seven. Sixty-three years had passed since she published her first Carolyn Keene mystery and forty years since she published her last.

In *Rediscovering Nancy Drew*, a chronicle of this conference, Carolyn Stewart Dyer writes that as a result of the conference and the media attention it attracted, Mildred Wirt Benson was the Person of the Week on ABC News, featured on numerous other TV and radio networks as well as in newspapers all around the world, named to the Women's Hall of Fame in both Ohio and Iowa, and given a Distinguished Alumni Award by the University of Iowa. Mildred Wirt Benson was an overnight sensation, sixty-three years in the making.

In 1958, Grosset & Dunlap decided to revise and reissue all the Nancy Drew and Hardy Boys titles published up to that point. The original novels stuck to a twenty-five-chapter formula, and the plan was to rewrite or revise every book into a twenty-chapter format. This was a huge undertaking, and a number of reasons have been offered for the decision to do this.

In his essay "The Nancy Drew *Myth*tery Stories," James Keeline asserts that the revisions were primarily undertaken for financial reasons. He notes that the printing process for the earlier books was expensive and outdated compared to photo-offset printing, a new method available in the 1950s that made it more affordable to produce, store, and alter texts. He states, "However, to move the old stories to the new method would cost the same as writing a completely new story that might be even more relevant to the modern readers."[3]

In *Girl Sleuth*, Rehak mentions the continued success of the series: "In 1959 the year's sales for the thirty-six volumes in the Nancy Drew series would be close to one and a half million."[4] I find this noteworthy because the publisher likely would not have pursued any revisions or repackaging for a less profitable series. Rehak also considers the cultural and historical events of this time, most notably that since as early as 1948, Grosset & Dunlap had been receiving more and more letters from concerned readers unhappy with "the prejudice and racism they saw scattered throughout the Syndicate books, in the form of uneducated dialect for all the foreign or non-Caucasian characters and villains who were invariably from these same two groups."[5] The publisher decided to remove the racist and stereo-typical content as part of the revisions to the originals.

Harriet Stratemeyer Adams oversaw the revisions and often did the writing herself. Unfortunately, her approach to addressing the racist elements was to eliminate any reference to characters of color. The changes she made sometimes introduced racism in new and subtler, but equally problematic, ways. For example, in *The Secret of the Old Clock*, Harriet turned Jeff Tucker, the Black caretaker who had been portrayed as inebriated and unreliable, with a police record, into a white caretaker. However, she also modified his character to be a responsible and upstanding citizen.

In addition to addressing racist elements, the stories were modified in other ways. Nancy became eighteen instead of sixteen. Her roadster became a convertible. The stories were also sometimes updated to incorporate con-temporary issues. In a few cases, this meant the revision had virtually no similarities to its earlier version. James Keeline gives the example of *The Mystery at the Moss-Covered Mansion*, which was in 1941 "originally a story about stolen heirlooms and became a 1971 story about stolen missile parts at Cape Canaveral and includes an infa-mous scene with exploding oranges."[6] The revised editions were given a new look too, with yellow spines and illustrated covers.

The last title in the original Nancy Drew Mystery Stories is *The Thirteenth Pearl*, released in 1979; however, the series continued in a new format with a different publisher. Simon & Schuster published these volumes up to number 175, *Werewolf in a Winter Wonderland*, released in 2003. And Nancy Drew has continued to have her stories told in other series, including the Nancy Drew Files, Nancy Drew Notebooks, Nancy Drew: Girl Detective, and Nancy Drew and the Clue Crew. Nancy Drew Diaries, the latest series from Simon & Schuster, debuted in 2013 and continues to release new titles as of this printing. There have also been a number of Nancy Drew movies and TV shows, including the recent *Nancy Drew* series on The CW, the graphic novel series by Dynamite Entertainment and Papercutz, and a popular chain of Nancy Drew computer games produced by Her Interactive.

Nancy Drew has been with us for nearly one hundred years, and while her evolution has not been without controversy, she undoubtedly changed the landscape of gender equality. Nancy Drew was a feminist before her time, providing an example to all readers of a self-reliant girl who could hold her own with anyone, who used her smarts to save herself and others, and who was in charge of her life, roaring down the road in her blue roadster and leaving a path for future generations of women to follow.

NOTES

1. Melanie Rehak, *Girl Sleuth: Nancy Drew and the Women Who Created Her* (Orlando, FL: Harcourt, 2008), 292.

2. Rehak, *Girl Sleuth*, 294–95.

3. James Keeline, "The Nancy Drew *Myth*tery Stories," in *Nancy Drew and Her Sister Sleuths: Essays on the Fiction of Girl Detectives*, ed. Michael G. Cornelius and Melanie E. Gregg (Jefferson, NC: McFarland, 2008), 29.

4. Rehak, *Girl Sleuth*, 242.

5. Rehak, *Girl Sleuth*, 243.

6. Keeline, "The Nancy Drew *Myth*tery Stories," 30.

⇾ RESOURCES ⇽

BOOKS

Cornelius, Michael G., and Melanie E. Gregg, eds. *Nancy Drew and Her Sister Sleuths: Essays on the Fiction of Girl Detectives.* Jefferson, NC: McFarland, 2008.

Dyer, Carolyn Stewart, and Nancy Tillman Romalov. *Rediscovering Nancy Drew.* Iowa City: University of Iowa Press, 1995.

Inness, Sherrie A. *Nancy Drew and Company: Culture, Gender, and Girls' Series.* Bowling Green, OH: Bowling Green State University Popular Press, 1997.

Kismaric, Carole, and Marvin Heiferman. *The Mysterious Case of Nancy Drew & the Hardy Boys.* New York: Simon & Schuster, 1998.

Rehak, Melanie. *Girl Sleuth: Nancy Drew and the Women Who Created Her.* Orlando, FL: Harcourt, 2008.

Rubini, Julie. *Missing Millie Benson: The Secret Case of the Nancy Drew Ghostwriter and Journalist.* Athens: Ohio University Press, 2015.

WEBSITES

Edward Stratemeyer & the Stratemeyer Syndicate. https://stratemeyer.org.

"Girls' Series Books Rediscovered: Nancy Drew and Friends." University of Maryland. https://exhibitions.lib.umd.edu/nancy/influential-authors/stratemeyer-syndicate.

"The Mysterious Mildred Benson." University of Iowa Libraries Iowa Women's Archives. https://www.lib.uiowa.edu /iwa/mildred.

The Nancy Drew Sleuth Unofficial Website created and maintained by Jennifer Fisher. https://www.nancy drewsleuth.com.

ARTICLES AND ESSAYS

Brown, Patricia Leigh. "Conversations/Mildred Benson: A Ghostwriter and Her Sleuth: 63 Years of Smarts and Gumption." *New York Times*, May 9, 1993.

———. "Nancy Drew: 30's Sleuth, 90's Role Model." *New York Times*, April 19, 1993.

Ferriss, Jeannie A. "A Sleuth of Our Own: A Historical View of Nancy Drew, Girl Detective," *SLIS Connecting* 3, no. 1 (2014): article 7. https://aquila.usm.edu/cgi/viewcon tent.cgi?article=1057&context=slisconnecting.

Lapin, Geoffrey S. "The Ghost of Nancy Drew," *Books at Iowa* 50, no. 1 (1989): 8–27. doi: https://doi.org/10.17077/0006 -7474.1164.

Rehak, Melanie. "Our Teenage Heroine at 75." *New York Times*, April 24, 2005.

Ruggierello, Andrea. "The Not-So-Hidden Racism of Nancy Drew," Electric Lit, September 6, 2018. https://electriclit erature.com/the-not-so-hidden-racism-of-nancy-drew.

VIDEO

Timonere, Shirley, executive producer. *Toledo Stories*. "The Storied Life of Millie Benson." Aired March 4, 2004, on WGTE Public Broadcasting. https://www.pbs.org/video /the-storied-life-of-millie-benson-t6rwna.

⋙ ACKNOWLEDGMENTS ⋘

In writing a book about the legacy of Nancy Drew, it's hard not to reflect on the many women who have profoundly influenced me, and I feel fortunate that so many come to mind.

This book would not exist without two in particular: my agent, Ammi-Joan Paquette, and my editor and publisher, Christy Ottaviano. Joan, thank you for your steady support and guidance. Christy, thank you for being enthusiastic about this story when it was a wisp of an idea and for helping me shape it into what it is today. I love working with both of you.

Thank you to the team at Little, Brown Books for Young Readers for all the care and attention you have given this book, and a special thanks to Sarah Watts and Vesper Stamper for your wonderful artwork.

The Laing Family won a school auction to name a future character in one of my books. They chose Maizy or Max, after their family's beloved cats, and I couldn't resist using both.

Many people helped me get details right in this book. Several friends shared their expertise in a variety of areas, and I especially want to thank Lisa Evans, Ann Kodani, Sammie Peng, and Katherine Rothschild for the time they took to help me. I have so much respect and appreciation for Melanie Rehak, not only for writing the excellent *Girl Sleuth: Nancy Drew and the Women Who Created Her*, but for reviewing my story. And thank you as well to copyeditor Erica Ferguson, who helped me catch mistakes.

The children's writing community is filled with many inspiring and kind people who have helped me in various ways. A special thank-you to my beloved writing groups for reading and deliberating different iterations of this book: the Rocket Cats—Ann Braden, Tara Dairman, and Elaine Vickers; and the Writing Roosters—Tracy Abell, Vanessa Appleby, Claudia Mills, Laura Perdew, Jennifer Simms, and our angel Michelle Begley. Additionally, Karina Yan Glaser, K. A. Holt, Shannon Ledger, Jeannie Mobley, Rachel Rodriguez, Katherine Rothschild, and Jennifer Stewart helped me sort out my thoughts on various drafts as I worked on this book over the years.

My writing and this book also benefited from Victoria Hanley and my classmates in her Lighthouse Writers workshop, the Better Books Marin conference, Anna-Maria Crum and Hilari Bell and their Plot Doctors service, an abundance of SCBWI workshops and conferences, virtual events hosted by the Writing Barn, and the ever-supportive EMLA community.